The Son of Seven Queens & Other Stories

Publications from
The Scheherazade Foundation

The Secrets of Scheherazade
An Ordered Experience
Tale of a Lantern & Other Stories
The Elephant & The Tortoise & Other Stories
The Monkey's Fiddle & Other Stories
Ghost of the Violet Well & Other Stories
Many Wise Fools & Other Stories
The Frog Prince & Other Stories
The Three Lemons & Other Stories
The Twelve-Headed Griffin & Other Stories
The Antelope Boy & Other Stories
Why the Fish Laughed & Other Stories
Two Cats & Other Stories
Three Stories
The Twilight of the Gods & Other Stories
The Son of Seven Queens & Other Stories
The Moon Maiden & Other Stories
The Metamorphosis & Other Stories
The Celestial Sisters & Other Stories
Tales from the Arabian Nights I
East of the Sun, West of the Moon & Other Stories
The Well at the End of the World & Other Stories

The Son of Seven Queens & Other Stories

Edited & Introduced by

TAHIR SHAH

The Scheherazade Foundation

The Scheherazade Foundation CIC
85 Great Portland Street
London
W1W 7LT
United Kingdom
www.SF.Charity
info@SF.Charity

First published by The Scheherazade Foundation CIC, 2023

THE SON OF SEVEN QUEENS
&
OTHER STORIES

A CIP catalogue record for this title is available from the British Library.

The Son of Seven Queens
Indian Fairy Tales
Joseph Jacobs
G. P. Putnam's Sons
1910

Bougoodoogahdah the Rain-bird
Folklore of the Noongahburrahs as Told to the Piccaninnies
Mrs. K. Langloh Parker
David Nutt Ltd.
1896

The Old Dog
Cossack Folk Tales
R. Nisbet Bain
George G. Harrap & Co.
1916

How Night Came
Fairy Tales from Brazil
Elsie Spicer Eells
Dodd, Mead & Co.
1917

Why the Moon Waxes & Wanes
A Treasury of Eskimo Tales
Clara Kern Bayliss
Thomas Y. Crowell Co.
1922

The Parsley Queen
Child Life in Japan
M. Chaplin Ayrton
D.C. Heath & Co.
1901

Prince Lindworm
East of the Sun & West of the Moon
Peter Christen Asbjørnsen & Jørgen Engebretsen Moe
George H. Doran Co.
1922

Adventures of the Beggar's Son
Oriental Folklore & Legends
Charles John Tibbitts
W. W. Gibbings Ltd.
1889

The Charmed Ring
Indian Fairy Tales
Joseph Jacobs
J. P. Putnum's & Son
1910

The King & the Ju Ju Tree
Folk-Stories from Southern Nigeria
Elphinstone Dayrell
Longmans, Green & Co.
1910

Childe Rowland
English Fairy Tales
Joseph Jacobs
G. P. Putnam's Sons
1892

The Weaver's Son & the Giant of the White Hill
Myths and Folklore of Ireland
Jeremiah Curtin
1890
Sampson Low & Co.

The Werewolf
The Swedish Fairy Book
Clara Stroebe
Frederick A. Stokes & Co.
1921

The Toad-woman
The Indian Fairy Book
Cornelius Mathews
Allen Brothers Inc.
1869

The Star Lovers
Green Willow & Other Japanese Fairy Tales
Grace James
Macmillan & Co.
1912

The Cobbler of Burgos
Tales from the Lands of Nuts & Grapes
Charles Sellers
Simpkin, Marshall & Co.
1888

The Plant of Life
Old French Fairy Tales
Comtesse de Ségur
1920
The Penn Publishing Co.

A CIP catalogue record for this title is available from the British Library.

ISBN 978-1-915311-43-6

Contents

Series Introduction

From earliest childhood, I was told stories.

Of course, I was – most children are told stories.

After all, telling children stories is one of the foundations that makes their early experiences a childhood.

But as I think back to the first years of my own life, I find myself reeling from the sheer quantity of stories my infant ears took in.

Whereas other children my age were told stories for amusement, my parents (and the people they associated with) recounted the endless streams of tales for a different reason.

In their opinion, stories – and the ability to tell them – were part of an ancient alchemy… a way of processing complex ideas, of solving problems, and of developing the human mind.

My father, the writer and thinker Idries Shah, believed that folklore was the single most important breakthrough ever developed by the human species. The way he saw it, the rise of stories was as consequential as the development of the languages in which they were told.

He would say that, without stories and storytelling, humanity would never have evolved in the way that it has – and that the folktales, which form a bedrock of ancient societies, are more precious than any physical artefact unearthed on an archaeological dig.

As the years of my own childhood slipped by, I found myself unbothered to work out the hidden layers within treasuries of stories – what my father called 'instruction manuals to the world'. Like everyone else, I simply absorbed the individual tales, delighting in them.

And that's it – the key point, the genius of stories and storytelling.

It's a thing I only grasped in adulthood… something that fascinates me deeply.

In the same way you can jump into a car and drive across the country without giving a second thought to the engine or how it works, you can appreciate stories without understanding the hidden layers and devices that make them what they are.

Stories are all around us.

They're in the TV and movies we so adore, in the video games we play, and of course in the books we read. They're in newspapers and magazines, too; in the conversations we share with old friends, and with new ones. They're on our mobile phones, in aeroplanes, in submarines, and even in our dreams.

Our obsession with, and craving for, stories rests squarely with the way we are so absorbed by them, just as it does with the way we don't need to continually consider how and why they work.

Throughout my life, I've devoted an increasing amount of time to gathering stories from all corners of the world.

It began in my late teens, when I began to criss-cross the continents in a crazed preoccupation with folklore. I developed a first-hand love affair with societies that, over millennia, gave birth to their own astonishing traditions of stories and storytelling.

Most of the time, when reading or listening to stories, we forget that these tales have been shaped through the passage of time. Like pebbles in a river smoothed by rushing waters, they were honed through centuries of telling and retelling.

When I was twelve years old, my father published a masterwork, *World Tales*. The first edition was very large and featured hundreds of original illustrations. The book was unlike any that had come before, for it detailed the provenance and history of each story told.

At bedtime one night, he presented me with an advanced copy. For as long as I could remember, my father had been talking about the project.

Having an actual copy in my hands at last was thrilling beyond words.

Peering down at me sternly, my father said:

'This is far more than a book, Tahir Jan. It's the foundation stone of a great building… a building that *is* human culture. As you grow older, and as you go out into the world, you will understand that the folklores contained between the covers of *World Tales* have brought amusement and educated, and have solved problems when they were needed most of all.'

My father was right.

When I eventually headed out into the wilds of the world for the first time, I discovered the stories contained in *World Tales* for myself, along with a great many more. Just as he said, the stories published in his treasury were the warp and weft threads of society. Stories are the matrix on which culture itself is based – a framework that enables daily life to continue as smoothly as it does.

In this series of books, we have drawn together stories from all over the world. It's a mission begun decades ago by *World Tales*.

Some of the pieces will be known to you, and others will not.

Some will be easy to comprehend, while others will be challenging, or even nonsensical.

I'd now like to note something else…

The Occidental world seems to assume stories must appear in certain regimented ways – presented with a well-defined beginning, a middle, and an end. You know what I mean: the protagonist winning against all odds, and the happy ending to it all.

In the ancient tradition of teaching stories, the kind recounted for an eternity around campfires in the desert and in longhouses deep in the jungle, there's no such standardisation.

Rather, there's usually a hotchpotch of conflicting threads: stories without a straight linear narrative but with an underlying turbulence that gets the reader, or the listener, to sit up and think.

At The Scheherazade Foundation, we are preoccupied with the way we can extract knowledge from stories – either deliberately, or in a less structured way.

We hold the firm opinion that, in order to remove the marrow from the bone stories are best served up in the way as they were passed from one generation to the next throughout human history.

In this series, we have drawn together tales that were gathered in particular during the nineteenth and early twentieth centuries. Spanning a vast range of cultures, they offer an extraordinary glimpse into the societies from which they are drawn – societies that were often changed shortly afterwards by social upheaval, technologies, and war.

Indeed, the fact any of them were recorded at all is a thing of wonder.

Intriguingly, some of the tales will now appear dated because vocabulary and writing styles have altered. But the fact that they seem old-fashioned is of great interest – proof of the way stories are constantly changing and evolving from one era to the next.

Over the last thirty years, I've gathered hundreds of tales on my own journeys, most of them spoken directly into my ears by storytellers and fellow travellers, by wizened old men in the middle of nowhere, and by anyone else good enough to indulge my pleas.

On all those zigzagging adventures, one story sticks out, tantalising me whenever I turn it around my head.

It was called 'The Man Who Turned into a Cat'.

The reason I mention it here is not because it was an especially fine tale, but rather because, from that moment, it affected the way I perceive the world.

It was as though I were a lock and that, by hearing the tale, a key had been slipped into me and turned.

Since first receiving it, I've never been quite the same, my state of consciousness having been flipped inside out.

The fellow traveller who recounted 'The Man Who Turned into a Cat' was lost in shadow, no more than a fragment of his left cheek protruding shyly into the light.

We were sitting on low divans in a teahouse in the ancient Afghan city of Herat.

When the tale had been whispered, I sat there in silence for a long while.

'What have you done to me?' I asked after a long pause.

The fellow traveller offered half a smile.

'*I* didn't do anything,' he replied. 'It's the story that's affected you – a story that I myself first heard when I was a child playing in the orchards of Balkh.'

Peering into the shadow, my eyes widened.

'I don't understand,' I said feebly. 'After all, it's not an especially grand story. There wasn't even a jinn.'

The traveller's mouth eased out from the shadows.

Very slowly, it grinned.

'Tales containing the greatest sustenance for a soul speak in the softest voice,' he said.

Tahir Shah

The Son of Seven Queens

Once upon a time, there lived a king who had seven queens, but no children. This was a great grief to him, especially when he remembered that on his death there would be no heir to inherit the kingdom.

Now it happened one day that a poor old fakir came to the king, and said, 'Your prayers are heard, your desire shall be accomplished, and one of your seven queens shall bear a son.'

The king's delight at this promise knew no bounds, and he gave orders for appropriate festivities to be prepared against the coming event throughout the length and breadth of the land.

Meanwhile the seven queens lived luxuriously in a splendid palace, attended by hundreds of female slaves, and fed to their hearts' content on sweetmeats and confectionery.

Now, the king was very fond of hunting, and one day, before he started, the seven queens sent him a message saying, 'May it please our dearest lord not to hunt towards the north today, for we have dreamt bad dreams, and fear lest evil should befall you.'

The king, to allay their anxiety, promised regard for their wishes, and set out towards the south; but as luck would have it, although he hunted diligently, he found no game. Nor had he more success to the east or west, so that, being a keen sportsman, and determined not to go home empty-handed, he forgot all about his promise, and turned to the north.

Here also, he was at first unsuccessful, but just as he had made up his mind to give up for that day, a white hind with golden horns and silver hooves flashed past him into a thicket. So quickly did it pass that he scarcely saw it; nevertheless, a burning desire to capture and possess the beautiful strange creature filled his breast.

He instantly ordered his attendants to form a ring round the thicket, and so encircle the hind; then, gradually narrowing the circle, he pressed forward till he could distinctly see the white hind panting in the midst. Nearer and nearer he advanced, till, just as he thought to lay hold of the beautiful strange creature, it gave one mighty bound, leapt clean over the king's head, and fled towards the mountains. Forgetful of all else, the king, setting spurs to his horse, followed at full speed.

On and on, he galloped, leaving his retinue far behind, keeping the white hind in view, never drawing bridle, until, finding himself in a narrow ravine with no outlet, he reined in his steed. Before him stood a miserable hovel, into which, being tired after his long, unsuccessful chase, he entered to ask for a drink of water.

An old woman, seated in the hut at a spinning-wheel, answered his request by calling to her daughter, and immediately from an inner room came a maiden so lovely and charming, so white-skinned and golden-haired, that the king was transfixed by astonishment at seeing so beautiful a sight in the wretched hovel.

She held the vessel of water to the king's lips, and as he drank, he looked into her eyes, and then it became clear to him that the girl was no other than the white hind with the golden horns and silver feet he had chased so far.

Her beauty bewitched him, so he fell on his knees, begging her to return with him as his bride; but she only laughed, saying seven queens were quite enough even for a king to manage. However, when he would take no refusal, but implored her to have pity on him, promising her everything she could desire, she replied, 'Give me the eyes of your seven queens, and then perhaps I may believe you mean what you say.'

The king was so carried away by the glamour of the white hind's magical beauty that he went home at once, had the eyes of his seven queens taken out, and, after throwing the poor blind creatures into a noisome dungeon whence they could not escape, set off once more for the hovel in the ravine, bearing with him his horrible offering. But the white hind only laughed cruelly when she saw the fourteen eyes and, threading them as a necklace, flung it round her mother's neck, saying, 'Wear that, little mother, as a keepsake, whilst I am away in the king's palace.'

Then she went back with the bewitched monarch as his bride, and he gave her the seven queens' rich clothes and jewels to wear, the seven queens' palace to live in, and the seven queens' slaves to wait upon her; so that she really had everything even a witch could desire.

Now, very soon after the seven wretched hapless queens had their eyes torn out, and were cast into prison, a baby was born to the youngest of the queens. It was a handsome boy, but the other queens were very jealous that the youngest amongst them should be so fortunate.

But, though at first they disliked the handsome little boy, he soon proved so useful to them, that ere long they all looked on him as their son. Almost as soon as he could walk about, he began scraping at the mud wall of their dungeon, and in an incredibly short space of time had made a hole big enough for him to crawl through. Through this he disappeared, returning in an hour or so laden with sweetmeats, which he divided equally amongst the seven blind queens.

As he grew older, he enlarged the hole, and slipped out two or three times every day to play with the little nobles in the town. No one knew who the tiny boy was, but everybody liked him, and he was so full of funny tricks and antics, so merry and bright, that he was sure to be rewarded by some girdle-cakes, a handful of parched grain, or some sweetmeats. All these things he brought home to his seven mothers, as he loved to call the seven blind queens, who by his help lived on in their dungeon when all the world thought they had starved to death ages before.

At last, when he was quite a big lad, he one day took his bow and arrow and went out to seek for game. Coming by chance past the palace where the white hind lived in wicked splendour and magnificence, he saw some pigeons fluttering around the white marble turrets and, taking good aim, shot one dead. It came tumbling past the very window where the white queen was sitting; she rose to see what was the matter and looked out. At the first glance of the handsome young lad standing there bow in hand, she knew by witchcraft that it was the king's son.

She nearly died of envy and spite, determining to destroy the lad without delay; therefore, sending a servant to bring him to her presence, she asked him if he would sell her the pigeon he had just shot.

'No,' replied the sturdy lad, 'the pigeon is for my seven blind mothers, who live in the noisome dungeon, and who would die if I did not bring them food.'

'Poor souls!' cried the cunning white witch; 'would you not like to bring them their eyes again? Give me the pigeon, my dear, and I faithfully promise to show you where to find them.'

Hearing this, the lad was delighted beyond measure, and gave up the pigeon at once. Whereupon the white queen told him to seek her mother without delay and ask for the eyes which she wore as a necklace.

'She will not fail to give them,' said the cruel queen, 'if you show her this token on which I have written what I want done.'

So, saying, she gave the lad a piece of broken potsherd, with these words inscribed on it: 'Kill the bearer at once and sprinkle his blood like water!'

Now, as the son of seven queens could not read, he took the fatal message cheerfully, and set off to find the white queen's mother.

Whilst he was journeying be passed through a town where every one of the inhabitants looked so sad that he could not help asking what was the matter. They told him it was because the king's only daughter refused to marry; so, when her father died there would be no heir to the throne.

They greatly feared she must be out of her mind, for though every good-looking young man in the kingdom had been shown to her, she declared she would only marry one who was the son of seven mothers, and who ever heard of such a thing? The king, in despair, had ordered every man who entered the city gates to be led before the princess; so, much to the lad's impatience, for he was in an immense hurry to find his mothers' eyes, he was dragged into the presence-chamber.

No sooner did the princess catch sight of him than she blushed and, turning to the king, said, 'Dear father, this is my choice!'

Never were such rejoicings as these few words produced.

The inhabitants nearly went wild with joy, but the son of seven queens said he would not marry the princess unless they first let him recover his mothers' eyes. When the beautiful bride heard his story, she asked to see the potsherd, for she was very learned and clever. Seeing the treacherous words, she said nothing, but taking another similar-shaped bit of potsherd, she wrote on it these words: 'Take care of this lad, giving him all he desires,' and returned it to the son of seven queens, who, none the wiser, set off on his quest.

Ere long, he arrived at the hovel in the ravine where the white witch's mother, a hideous old creature, grumbled dreadfully on reading the message, especially when the lad asked for the necklace of eyes. Nevertheless, she took it off, and gave it him, saying, 'There are only thirteen of 'em now, for I lost one last week.'

The lad, however, was only too glad to get any at all, so he hurried home as fast as he could to his seven mothers and gave two eyes apiece to the six elder queens; but to the youngest he gave one, saying, 'Dearest little mother! – I will be your other eye always!'

After this, he set off to marry the princess, as he had promised, but when passing by the white queen's palace he saw some pigeons on the roof. Drawing his bow, he shot one, and it came fluttering past the window. The white hind looked out, and lo! There was the king's son alive and well.

She cried with hatred and disgust but, sending for the lad, asked him how he had returned so soon, and when she heard how he had brought home the thirteen eyes, and given them to the seven blind queens, she could hardly restrain her rage.

Nevertheless, she pretended to be charmed with his success, and told him that if he would give her this pigeon also, she would reward him with the yogi's wonderful cow, whose milk flows all day long, and makes a pond as big as a kingdom. The lad, nothing loth, gave her the pigeon; whereupon, as before, she bade him go ask her mother for the cow, and gave him a potsherd whereon was written: 'Kill this lad without fail and sprinkle his blood like water!'

But on the way, the son of seven queens looked in on the princess, just to tell her how he came to be delayed, and she, after reading the message on the potsherd, gave him another in its stead; so that when the lad reached the old hag's hut and asked her for the yogi's cow, she could not refuse, but told the boy how to find it; and bidding him of all things not to be afraid of the eighteen thousand demons who kept watch and ward over the treasure, told him to be off before she became too angry at her daughter's foolishness in thus giving away so many good things.

Then the lad did as he had been told bravely. He journeyed on and on till he came to a milk-white pond, guarded by the eighteen thousand demons. They were really frightful to behold but, plucking up courage, he whistled a tune as he walked through them, looking neither to the right nor the left.

By-and-by he came upon the yogi's cow, tall, white, and beautiful, while the yogi himself, who was king of all the demons, sat milking her day and night, and the milk streamed from her udder, filling the milk-white tank.

The yogi, seeing the lad, called out fiercely, 'What do you want here?'

Then the lad answered, according to the old hag's bidding, 'I want your skin, for king Indra is making a new kettle-drum, and says your skin is nice and tough.'

Upon this, the yogi began to shiver and shake (for no jinn or yogi dares disobey king Indra's command) and, falling at the lad's feet, cried, 'If you will spare me I will give you anything I possess, even my beautiful white cow!'

To this, the son of seven queens, after a little pretended hesitation, agreed, saying that after all it would not be difficult to find a nice tough skin like the yogi's elsewhere; so, driving the wonderful cow before him, he set off homewards. The seven queens were delighted to possess so marvellous an animal, and though they toiled from morning till night making curds and whey, besides selling milk to the confectioners, they could not use half the cow gave, and became richer and richer day by day.

Seeing them so comfortably off, the son of seven queens started with a light heart to marry the princess; but when passing the white hind's palace, he could not resist sending a bolt at some pigeons which were cooing on the parapet. One fell dead just beneath the window where the white queen was sitting. Looking out, she saw the lad hale and hearty standing before her and grew whiter than ever with rage and spite.

She sent for him to ask how he had returned so soon, and when she heard how kindly her mother had received him, she very nearly had a fit; however, she dissembled her feelings as well as she could and, smiling sweetly, said she was glad to have been able to fulfil her promise, and that if he would give her this third pigeon, she would do yet more for him than she had done before, by giving him the million-fold rice, which ripens in one night.

The lad was of course delighted at the very idea, and, giving up the pigeon, set off on his quest, armed as before with a potsherd, on which was written, 'Do not fail this time. Kill the lad and sprinkle his blood like water!'

But when he looked in on his princess, just to prevent her becoming anxious about him, she asked to see the potsherd as usual, and substituted another, on which was written, 'Yet again give this lad all he requires, for his blood shall be as your blood!'

Now when the old hag saw this, and heard how the lad wanted the million-fold rice which ripens in a single night, she fell into the most furious rage, but being terribly afraid of her daughter, she controlled herself, and bade the boy go and find the field guarded by eighteen millions of demons, warning him on no account to look back after having plucked the tallest spike of rice, which grew in the centre.

So, the son of seven queens set off, and soon came to the field where, guarded by eighteen millions of demons, the million-fold rice grew. He walked on bravely, looking neither to the right or left, till he reached the centre and plucked the tallest ear, but as he turned homewards a thousand sweet voices rose behind him, crying in tenderest accents, 'Pluck me too! oh, please pluck me too!'

He looked back, and lo! There was nothing left of him but a little heap of ashes!

Now as time passed by and the lad did not return, the old hag grew uneasy, remembering the message 'his blood shall be as your blood'; so, she set off to see what had happened.

Soon she came to the heap of ashes and, knowing by her arts what it was, she took a little water and, kneading the ashes into a paste, formed it into the likeness of a man; then, putting a drop of blood from her little finger into its mouth, she blew on it, and instantly the son of seven queens started up as well as ever.

'Don't you disobey orders again!' grumbled the old hag, 'or next time I'll leave you alone. Now be off, before I repent of my kindness!'

So, the son of seven queens returned joyfully to his seven mothers, who, by the aid of the million-fold rice, soon became the richest people in the kingdom. Then they celebrated their son's marriage to the clever princess with all imaginable pomp; but the bride was so clever, she would not rest until she had made known her husband to his father and punished the wicked white witch.

She made her husband build a palace exactly like the one in which the seven queens had lived, and in which the white witch now dwelt in splendour. Then, when all was prepared, she bade her husband give a grand feast to the king.

Now, the king had heard much of the mysterious son of seven queens and his marvellous wealth, so he gladly accepted the invitation; but what was his astonishment when on entering the palace he found it was a facsimile of his own in every particular! And when his host, richly attired, led him straight to the private hall, where on royal thrones sat the seven queens, dressed as he had last seen them, he was speechless with surprise, until the princess, coming forward, threw herself at his feet, and told him the whole story.

Then the king awoke from his enchantment, and his anger rose against the wicked white hind who had bewitched him so long, until he could not contain himself. So, she was put to death, and her grave ploughed over, and after that the seven queens returned to their own splendid palace, and everybody lived happily.

From: *Indian Fairy Tales*

Why the Moon Waxes & Wanes

In a certain village on the Yukon River there once lived four brothers and a sister. The sister's companion was the youngest boy, of whom she was very fond. This boy was lazy and could never be made to work. The other brothers were great hunters and in the autumn, they hunted at sea, for they lived near the shore.

As soon as the Bladder feast in December was over, they went to the mountains and hunted reindeer. The boy never went with them, but remained at home with his sister, and they amused each other.

One time, however, she became angry at him, and that night when she carried food to the other brothers in the assembly house where the men slept, she gave none to the youngest brother. When she went out of the assembly house, she saw a ladder leading up into the sky, with a line hanging down by the side of it. Taking hold of the line, she ascended the ladder, going up into the sky. As she was going up, the younger brother came out and, seeing her, at once ran back and called to his brothers: 'Our sister is climbing the sky! Our sister is climbing the sky!'

'Oh, you lazy youngster, why do you tell us that? She is doing no such thing,' said they.

'Come and see for yourselves! Come, quick!' he cried, very much excited.

Sure enough! Up she was going at a rapid rate.

The boy caught up his sealskin breeches and, being in a hurry, thrust one leg into them and then drew a deerskin sock on the other foot as he ran outside. There he saw the girl far away up in the sky and began at once to go up the ladder toward her; but she floated away, he following in turn.

The girl became the sun, and the boy became the moon, and ever since that time he pursues but never overtakes her. At night the sun sinks in the west, and the moon is seen coming up in the east to go circling after, but always too late.

The moon, being without food, wanes slowly away from starvation until it is quite lost to sight; then the sun reaches out and feeds it from the dish in which she carried food to the assembly house.

After the moon is fed and gradually brought to the full, it is permitted to starve again, thus producing the waxing and waning which we see every month.

From: A Treasury of Eskimo Tales

Bougoodoogahdah the Rain-bird

BOUGOODOOGAHDAH WAS AN old woman who lived alone with her four hundred dingoes.

From living so long with these dogs, she had grown not to care for her fellow creatures except as food. She and the dogs lived on human flesh, and it was her cunning which gained such food for them all.

She would sally forth from her camp with her two little dogs; she would be sure to meet some local fellows, probably twenty or thirty, going down to the creek. She would say, 'I can tell you where there are lots of paddy melons.'

They would ask where, and she would answer, 'Over there, on the point of that moorillah or ridge. If you will go there and have your nullahs ready, I will go with my two dogs and round them up towards you.'

The local fellows invariably stationed themselves where she had told them, and off went Bougoodoogahdah and her two dogs. But not to round up the paddy melons. She went quickly towards her camp, calling softly, 'Birree, gougou,' which meant 'Sool 'em, sool 'em,' and was the signal for the dogs to come out.

Quickly they came and surrounded the local fellows, took them by surprise, flew at them, bit and worried them to death. Then they and Bougoodoogahdah dragged the bodies to their camp. There they were cooked and were food for the old woman and the dogs for some time. As soon as the supply was finished, the same plan to obtain more was repeated.

The local fellows missed so many of their friends that they determined to find out what had become of them. They began to suspect the old woman who lived alone and hunted over the moorillahs with her two little dogs. They proposed that the next party that went to the creek should divide and some stay behind in hiding and watch what went on. Those watching saw the old woman advance towards their friends, talk to them for a while, and then go off with her two dogs. They saw their friends station themselves at the point of the moorillah or ridge, holding their nullahs in readiness, as if waiting for something to come. Presently they heard a low cry from the old woman of 'Birree gougou,' which cry was quickly followed by dingoes coming out of the bush in every direction, in hundreds, surrounding the local fellows at the point.

The dingoes closed in, quickly hemming the local fellows in all around; then they made a simultaneous rush at them, tore them with their teeth, and killed them.

The local fellows watching saw that when the dogs had killed their friends they were joined by the old woman, who helped them to drag off the bodies to their camp.

Having seen all this, back went the watchers to their tribe and told what they had seen. All the tribes round mustered up and decided to execute a swift vengeance. In order to do so, out they sallied well-armed. A detachment went on to entrap the dogs and Bougoodoogahdah. Then, just when the usual massacre of the locals was to begin and the dogs were closing in round them for the purpose, out rushed over two hundred local fellows, and so effectual was their attack that every dog was killed, as well as Bougoodoogahdah and her two little dogs.

The old woman lay where she had been slain, but as the locals went away, they heard her cry: 'Bougoodoogahdah.'

So back they went and broke her bones, first they broke her legs and then left her. But again, as they went, they heard her cry: 'Bougoodoogahdah.'

Then back again they came, and again, until at last, every bone in her body was broken, but still, she cried: 'Bougoodoogahdah.'

So, one man waited beside her to see whence came the sound, for surely, they thought, she must be dead. He saw her heart move and cry again: 'Bougoodoogahdah' and as it cried, out came a little bird from it.

This little bird runs on the moorillahs and calls at night: 'Bougoodoogahdah.'

All day it stays in one place, and only at night comes out. It is a little greyish bird, something like a weedah. The locals call it a rainmaker, for if any one steals its eggs, it cries out incessantly 'Bougoodoogahdah' until in answer to its call the rain falls.

And when the country is stricken with a drought, the locals look for one of these little birds and, finding it, chase it until it cries aloud: 'Bougoodoogahdah, Bougoodoogahdah' and when they hear its cry in the daytime, they know the rain will soon fall.

As the little bird flew from the heart of the woman, all the dead dingoes were changed into snakes, many different kinds, all poisonous. The two little dogs were changed into dayall minyah, a very small kind of carpet snake, non-poisonous, for these two little dogs had never bitten the locals as the other dogs had done.

At the points of the Moorillahs where Bougoodoogahdah and her dingoes used to slay the locals are heaps of white stones, which are supposed to be the fossilised bones of the massacred men.

From: Folklore of the Noongahburrahs
as Told to the Piccaninnies

The Parsley Queen

How curious that the daughter of a peasant dwelling in an obscure country village near Aska, in the province of Yamato should become a queen! Yet such was the case. Her father died while she was yet in her infancy, and the girl applied herself to the tending of her mother with all filial piety.

One day, when she had gone out in the fields to gather some parsley, of which her mother was very fond, it chanced that prince Shotoku, the great Buddhist teacher, was making a progress to his palace, and all the inhabitants of the countryside flocked to the road along which the procession was passing, in order to behold the gorgeous spectacle, and to show their respect for the Mikado's son.

The filial girl, alone, paying no heed to what was going on around her, continued picking her parsley. She was observed from his carriage by the prince, who, astonished at the circumstance, sent one of his retainers to inquire into its cause.

The girl replied, 'My mother bade me pick parsley, and I am following her instructions – that is the reason why I have not turned round to pay my respects to the prince.'

The latter being informed of her answer, was filled with admiration at the strictness of her filial piety. Alighting at her mother's cottage on the way back, he told her of the occurrence, and placing the girl in the next carriage to his own, took her home with him to the Imperial Palace, and ended by making her his wife, upon which the people, knowing her story, gave her the name of the 'Parsley Queen.'

From: Child Life in Japan

The Old Dog

THERE WAS ONCE a man who had a dog.

While the dog was young, he was made much of, but when he grew old, he was driven out of doors. So, he went and lay outside the fence, and a wolf came up to him and said, 'Doggy, why so down in the mouth?'

'While I was young,' said the dog, 'they made much of me; but now that I am old, they beat me.'

The wolf said, 'I see your master in the field; go after him, and perchance he'll give you something.'

'Nay,' said the dog, 'they won't even let me walk about the fields now, they only beat me.'

'Look now,' said the wolf, 'I'm sorry and will make things better for you. Your mistress, I see, has put her child down beneath that wagon. I'll seize it and make off with it. Run after me and bark, and though you have no teeth left, tousle me as much as you can, so that your mistress may see it.'

So, the wolf seized the child, and ran away with it, and the dog ran after him, and began to tousle him. His mistress saw it, and made after them with a harrow, crying at the same time, 'Husband, husband! the wolf has got the child! Gabriel, Gabriel! Don't you see? The wolf has got the child!'

Then the man chased the wolf and got back the child.

'Brave old dog!' said he; 'you are old and toothless, and yet you can give help in time of need and will not let your master's child be stolen.'

And henceforth, the woman and her husband gave the old dog a large lump of bread every day.

From: Cossack Folk Tales

Prince Lindworm

Once upon a time, there was a fine young *king* who was married to the loveliest of queens.

They were exceedingly happy, all but for one thing – they had no children. And this often made them both sad because the *queen* wanted a dear little child to play with, and the *king* wanted an heir to the kingdom.

One day the *queen* went out for a walk by herself, and she met an ugly old woman. The old woman was just like a witch: but she was a nice kind of witch, not the cantankerous sort.

She said, 'Why do you look so doleful, pretty lady?'

'It's no use my telling you,' answered the *queen*, 'nobody in the world can help me.'

'Oh, you never know,' said the old woman. 'Just you let me hear what your trouble is, and maybe I can put things right.'

'My dear woman, how can you?' said the *queen*. 'The *king* and I have no children: that's why I am so distressed.'

'Well, you needn't be,' said the old witch.

'I can set that right in a twinkling, if only you will do exactly as I tell you. Listen. Tonight, at sunset, take a little drinking cup with two ears' (that is, handles), 'and put it bottom upwards on the ground in the northwest corner of your garden. Then, go and lift it up tomorrow morning at sunrise, and you will find two roses underneath it, one red and one white. If you eat the red rose, a little boy will be born to you: if you eat the white rose, a little girl will be sent. But, whatever you do, you mustn't eat *both* the roses, or you'll be sorry, – that I warn you! Only one: remember that!'

'Thank you a thousand times,' said the *queen*, 'this is good news indeed!'

And she wanted to give the old woman her gold ring; but the old woman wouldn't take it.

So, the *queen* went home and did as she had been told: and next morning at sunrise she stole out into the garden and lifted up the little drinking-cup. She *was* surprised, for indeed she had hardly expected to see anything. But there were the two roses underneath it, one red and one white.

And now she was dreadfully puzzled, for she did not know which to choose.

'If I choose the red one,' she thought, 'and I have a little boy, he may grow up and go to the wars and get killed. But if I choose the white one, and have a little girl, she will stay at home awhile with us, but later on, she will get married and go away and leave us. So, whichever it is, we may be left with no child after all.'

However, at last she decided on the white rose, and she ate it. And it tasted so sweet that she took and ate the red one too – without ever remembering the old woman's solemn warning.

A little time after this, the *king* went away to the wars: and while he was still away, the *queen* became the mother of twins. One was a lovely baby boy, and the other was a *lindworm*, or Serpent. She was terribly frightened when she saw the *lindworm*, but he wriggled away out of the room, and nobody seemed to have seen him but herself: so that she thought it must have been a dream. The baby *prince* was so beautiful and so healthy, the *queen* was full of joy: and likewise, as you may suppose, was the *king* when he came home and found his son and heir. Not a word was said by anyone about the *lindworm*: only the *queen* thought about it now and then.

Many days and years passed by, and the baby grew up into a handsome young *prince*, and it was time that he got married. The *king* sent him off to visit foreign kingdoms, in the Royal coach, with six white horses, to look for a princess grand enough to be his wife. But at the very first crossroads, the way was stopped by an enormous *lindworm*, enough to frighten the bravest.

He lay in the middle of the road with a great wide-open mouth, and cried, 'A bride for me before a bride for you!'

Then the *prince* made the coach turn around and try another road: but it was all no use.

For, at the first crossways, there lay the *lindworm* again, crying out, 'A bride for me before a bride for you!'

So, the *prince* had to turn back home again to the castle, and give up his visits to the foreign kingdoms. And his mother, the *queen*, had to confess that what the *lindworm* said was true. For he was really the eldest of her twins: and so, he ought to have a wedding first.

There seemed nothing for it but to find a bride for the *lindworm*, if his younger brother, the *prince*, were to be married at all. So, the *king* wrote to a distant country, and asked for a princess to marry his son (but, of course, he didn't say which son), and presently a princess arrived. But she wasn't allowed to see her bridegroom until he stood by her side in the great hall and was married to her, and then, of course, it was too late for her to say she wouldn't have him. But next morning, the princess had disappeared. The *lindworm* lay sleeping all alone: and it was quite plain that he had eaten her.

A little while after, the prince decided that he might now go journeying again in search of a *princess*. And off he drove in the Royal chariot with the six white horses. But at the first crossways, there lay the *lindworm*, crying with his great wide-open mouth, 'A bride for me before a bride for you!'

So, the carriage tried another road, and the same thing happened, and they had to turn back again this time, just as formerly. And the king wrote to several foreign countries, to know if anyone would marry his son. At last, another *princess* arrived, this time from a very far distant land. And, of course, she was not allowed to see her future husband before the wedding took place, – and then, lo and behold! It was the *lindworm* who stood at her side. And next morning, the princess had disappeared and the *lindworm* lay sleeping all alone, and it was quite clear that he had eaten her.

By and by, the *prince* started on his quest for the third time: and at the first crossroads, there lay the *lindworm* with his great wide-open mouth, demanding a bride as before. And the *prince* went straight back to the castle and told the *king*: 'You must find another bride for my elder brother.'

'I don't know where I am to find her,' said the *king*, 'I have already made enemies of two great kings who sent their daughters here as brides: and I have no notion how I can obtain a third lady. People are beginning to say strange things, and I am sure no *princess* will dare to come.'

Now, down in a little cottage near a wood, there lived the *king's* shepherd, an old man with his only daughter. And the *king* came one day and said to him, 'Will you give me your daughter to marry my son the *lindworm*? And I will make you rich for the rest of your life.'

'No, sire,' said the shepherd, 'that I cannot do. She is my only child, and I want her to take care of me when I am old. Besides, if the *lindworm* would not spare two beautiful princesses, he won't spare her either. He will just gobble her up: and she is much too good for such a fate.'

But the *king* wouldn't take 'No' for an answer, and at last, the old man had to give in.

Well, when the old shepherd told his daughter that she was to be *Prince Lindworm's* bride, she was utterly in despair. She went out into the woods, crying and wringing her hands and bewailing her hard fate. And while she wandered to and fro, an old witch-woman suddenly appeared out of a big hollow oak-tree, and asked her, 'Why do you look so doleful, pretty lass?'

The shepherd-girl said, 'It's no use my telling you, for nobody in the world can help me.'

'Oh, you never know,' said the old woman. 'Just you let me hear what your trouble is, and maybe I can put things right.'

'Ah, how can you?' said the girl. 'For I am to be married to the *king's* eldest son, who is a *lindworm*. He has already married two beautiful princesses and devoured them: and he will eat me too! No wonder I am distressed.'

'Well, you needn't be,' said the witch-woman. 'All that can be set right in a twinkling: if only you will do exactly as I tell you.'

So, the girl said she would.

'Listen, then,' said the old woman. 'After the marriage ceremony is over, and when it is time for you to retire to rest, you must ask to be dressed in ten snow-white shifts. And you must then ask for a tub full of lye,' (that is, washing water prepared with wood-ashes) 'and a tub full of fresh milk, and as many whips as a boy can carry in his arms, – and have all these brought into your bedchamber. Then, when the *lindworm* tells you to shed a shift, do you bid him slough a skin. And when all his skins are off, you must dip the whips in the lye and whip him; next, you must wash him in the fresh milk; and, lastly, you must take him and hold him in your arms, if it's only for one moment.'

'The last is the worst notion – ugh!' said the shepherd's daughter, and she shuddered at the thought of holding the cold, slimy, scaly *lindworm*.

'Do just as I have said, and all will go well,' said the old woman. Then she disappeared again in the oak-tree.

When the wedding day arrived, the girl was fetched in the royal chariot with the six white horses and taken to the castle to be decked as a bride. And she asked for ten snow-white shifts to be brought her, and the tub of lye, and the tub of milk, and as many whips as a boy could carry in his arms.

The ladies and courtiers in the castle thought, of course, that this was some bit of peasant superstition, all rubbish and nonsense.

But the *king* said, 'Let her have whatever she asks for.'

She was then arrayed in the most wonderful robes and looked the loveliest of brides. She was led to the hall where the wedding ceremony was to take place, and she saw the *lindworm* for the first time as he came in and stood by her side. So, they were married, and a great wedding feast was held, a banquet fit for the son of a king.

When the feast was over, the bridegroom and bride were conducted to their apartment, with music, and torches, and a great procession. As soon as the door was shut, the *lindworm* turned to her and said, 'Fair maiden, shed a shift!'

The shepherd's daughter answered him, '*Prince Lindworm*, slough a skin!'

'No one has ever dared tell me to do that before!' said he.

'But I command you to do it now!' said she.

Then he began to moan and wriggle, and in a few minutes a long snakeskin lay upon the floor beside him. The girl drew off her first shift and spread it on top of the skin.

The *lindworm* said again to her, 'Fair maiden, shed a shift.'

The shepherd's daughter answered him, '*Prince Lindworm*, slough a skin.'

'No one has ever dared tell me to do that before,' said he.

'But I command you to do it now,' said she.

Then with groans and moans, he cast off the second skin, and she covered it with her second shift. The *lindworm* said for the third time, 'Fair maiden, shed a shift.'

The shepherd's daughter answered him again, '*Prince Lindworm*, slough a skin.'

'No one has ever dared tell me to do that before,' said he, and his little eyes rolled furiously.

But the girl was not afraid, and once more she commanded him to do as she bade.

And so, this went on until nine *lindworm* skins were lying on the floor, each of them covered with a snow-white shift. And there was nothing left of the *lindworm* but a huge thick mass, most horrible to see. Then, the girl seized the whips, dipped them in the lye, and whipped him as hard as ever she could. Next, she bathed him all over in the fresh milk. Lastly, she dragged him on to the bed and put her arms round him. And she fell fast asleep that very moment.

Next morning very early, the *king* and the courtiers came and peeped in through the keyhole. They wanted to know what had become of the girl, but none of them dared enter the room. However, in the end, growing bolder, they opened the door a tiny bit. And there they saw the girl, all fresh and rosy, and beside her lay – no *lindworm*, but the handsomest prince that anyone could wish to see.

The *king* ran out and fetched the *queen*, and after that, there were such rejoicings in the castle as never were known before or since. The wedding took place all over again, much finer than the first, with festivals and banquets and merrymakings for days and weeks. No bride was ever so beloved by a king and queen as this peasant maid from the shepherd's cottage.

There was no end to their love and their kindness towards her because, by her sense and her calmness and her courage, she had saved their son, *Prince Lindworm.*

From: East of the Sun & West of the Moon

How Night Came

YEARS AND YEARS ago, at the very beginning of time, when the world had just been made, there was no night. It was day all the time. No one had ever heard of sunrise or sunset, starlight or moonbeams. There were no night birds, nor night beasts, nor night flowers. There were no lengthening shadows, nor soft night air, heavy with perfume.

In those days, the daughter of the great sea serpent, who dwelt in the depths of the seas, married one of the sons of the great earth race known as Man. She left her home among the shades of the deep seas and came to dwell with her husband in the land of daylight. Her eyes grew weary of the bright sunlight and her beauty faded. Her husband watched her with sad eyes, but he did not know what to do to help her.

'O, if night would only come,' she moaned as she tossed about wearily on her couch. 'Here it is always day, but in my father's kingdom there are many shadows. O, for a little of the darkness of night!'

Her husband listened to her moaning. 'What is night?' he asked her. 'Tell me about it and perhaps I can get a little of it for you.'

'Night,' said the daughter of the great sea serpent, 'is the name we give to the heavy shadows which darken my father's kingdom in the depths of the seas. I love the sunlight of your earth land, but I grow very weary of it. If we could have only a little of the darkness of my father's kingdom to rest our eyes part of the time.'

Her husband at once called his three most faithful slaves. 'I am about to send you on a journey,' he told them. 'You are to go to the kingdom of the great sea serpent who dwells in the depths of the seas and ask him to give you some of the darkness of night that his daughter may not die here amid the sunlight of our earth land.'

The three slaves set forth for the kingdom of the great sea serpent. After a long dangerous journey, they arrived at his home in the depths of the seas and asked him to give them some of the shadows of night to carry back to the earth land. The great sea serpent gave them a big bag full at once. It was securely fastened, and the great sea serpent warned them not to open it until they were once more in the presence of his daughter, their mistress.

The three slaves started out, bearing the big bag full of night upon their heads. Soon, they heard strange sounds within the bag. It was the sound of the voices of all the night beasts, all the night birds, and all the night insects. If you have ever heard the night chorus from the jungles on the banks of the rivers, you will know how it sounded. The three slaves had never heard sounds like those in all their lives. They were terribly frightened.

'Let us drop the bag full of night right here where we are and run away as fast as we can,' said the first slave.

'We shall perish. We shall perish, anyway, whatever we do,' cried the second slave.

'Whether we perish or not, I am going to open the bag and see what makes all those terrible sounds,' said the third slave.

Accordingly, they laid the bag on the ground and opened it. Out rushed all the night beasts and all the night birds and all the night insects and out rushed the great black cloud of night. The slaves were more frightened than ever at the darkness and escaped to the jungle.

The daughter of the great sea serpent was waiting anxiously for the return of the slaves with the bag full of night.

Ever since they had started out on their journey, she had looked for their return, shading her eyes with her hand and gazing away off at the horizon, hoping with all her heart that they would hasten to bring the night. In that position, she was standing under a royal palm tree when the three slaves opened the bag and let night escape.

'Night comes. Night comes at last,' she cried, as she saw the clouds of night upon the horizon.

Then she closed her eyes and went to sleep there under the royal palm tree.

When she awoke, she felt greatly refreshed. She was once more the happy princess who had left her father's kingdom in the depths of the great seas to come to the earth land. She was now ready to see the day again. She looked up at the bright star shining above the royal palm tree and said, 'O, bright beautiful star, henceforth you shall be called the morning star and you shall herald the approach of day. You shall reign queen of the sky at this hour.'

Then she called all the birds about her and said to them, 'O, wonderful, sweet singing birds, henceforth I command you to sing your sweetest songs at this hour to herald the approach of day.'

The cock was standing by her side.

'You,' she said to him, 'shall be appointed the watchman of the night. Your voice shall mark the watches of the night and shall warn the others that the Madrugada comes.'

To this very day in Brazil, we call the early morning the Madrugada. The cock announces its approach to the waiting birds. The birds sing their sweetest songs at that hour and the morning star reigns in the sky as queen of the Madrugada.

When it was daylight again the three slaves crept home through the forests and jungles with their empty bag.

'O, faithless slaves,' said their master, 'why did you not obey the voice of the great sea serpent and open the bag only in the presence of his daughter, your mistress? Because of your disobedience, I shall change you into monkeys. Henceforth you shall live in the trees. Your lips shall always bear the mark of the sealing wax which sealed the bag full of night.'

To this very day, one sees the mark upon the monkeys' lips, where they bit off the wax which sealed the bag; and in Brazil night leaps out quickly upon the earth just as it leapt quickly out of the bag in those days at the beginning of time.

And all the night beasts and night birds and night insects give a sunset chorus in the jungles at nightfall.

From: Fairy Tales from Brazil

Adventures of the Beggar's Son

When the Son of the Chan arrived as before at the cold Forest of Death, he exclaimed with threatening gestures at the foot of the amiri-tree, 'You dead one, descend, or I will hew down the tree.'

Ssidi descended.

The son of Chan placed him in the sack, bound the sack fast with the rope, ate of his provender, and journeyed forth with his burden.

Then the dead one spoke these words, 'Since we have a long journey before us, do you relate a pleasant story by the way, or I will do so.'

But the Son of the Chan merely shook his head without speaking a word.

Whereupon Ssidi commenced the following tale: 'A long time ago, there was a mighty Chan who was ruler over a country full of marketplaces. At the source of the river which ran through it, there was an immense marsh, and in this marsh, there dwelt two crocodile-frogs, who would not allow the water to run out of the marsh. And because there came no water over their fields, every year did both the good and the bad have cause to mourn, until such times as a man had been given to the frogs for the pests to devour. And at length, the lot fell upon the Chan himself to be an offering to them, and needful as he was to the welfare of the kingdom, denial availed him not; therefore father and son communed sorrowfully together, saying, "Which of us two shall go?"

'"I am an old man," said the father, "and shall leave no one to lament me. I will go, therefore. Do you remain here, my son, and reign according as it is appointed."

'"O Tângâri," exclaimed the son, "verily this is not as it should be! You have brought me up with care, O my father! If the Chan and the wife of the Chan remain, what need is there of their son? I then will go and be as a feast for the frogs."

'Thus spoke he, and the people walked sorrowfully around about him, and then betook themselves back again. Now, the son of the Chan had for his companion the son of a poor man, and he went to him and said, "Walk ye according to the will of your parents, and remain at home in peace and safety. I am going, for the good of the kingdom, to serve as a sacrifice to the frogs."

'At these words the son of the poor man said, weeping and lamenting, "From my youth up, O Chan, thou hast carefully fostered me. I will go with you and share your fate."

'Then they both arose and went unto the frogs; and on the verge of the marsh, they heard the yellow frog and the blue frog conversing with one another. And the frogs said, "If the son of the Chan and his companion did but know that if they only smote off our heads with the sword, and the son of the Chan consumed me, the yellow frog, and the son of the poor man consumed thee, the blue frog, they would both cast out from their mouths gold and brass, then would the country be no longer compelled to find food for frogs."

'Now, because the son of the Chan understood all sorts of languages, he comprehended the discourse of the frogs, and he and his companion smote the heads of the frogs with their swords; and when they had devoured the frogs, they threw out from their mouths gold and brass at their heart's pleasure. Then said the wanderers, "The frogs are both slain – the course of the waters will be hemmed in no more. Let us then turn back unto our own country." But the son of the Chan agreed not to this, and said, "Let us not turn back into our own country, lest they say they are become spirits; therefore, it is better that we journey further."

'As they thereupon were walking over a mountain, they came to a tavern, in which dwelt two women, beautiful to behold – mother and daughter. Then said they, "We would buy strong liquor that we might drink."

'The women replied, "What have ye to give in exchange for strong liquor?"

'Thereupon each of them threw forth gold and brass, and the women found pleasure therein, admitted them into their dwelling, gave them liquor in abundance until they became stupid and slept, took from them what they had, and then turned them out of doors.

'Now when they awoke, the son of the Chan and his companion travelled along a river and arrived in a wood, where they found some children quarrelling one with another.

'"Wherefore," inquired they, "do you thus dispute?"

'"'We have,' said the children, 'found a cap in this wood, and everyone desires to possess it.'

'"Of what use is the cap?"

'"The cap has this wonderful property, that whosoever places it on his head can be seen neither by the Tângâri, nor by men, nor by the Tschadkurrs" (evil spirits).

'"Now go all of ye to the end of the forest and run hither and I will in the meanwhile keep the cap and give it to the first of you who reaches me." Thus spoke the son of the Chan; and the children ran, but they found not the cap, for it was upon the head of the Chan.

'"Even now it was here," said they, "and now it is gone." And after they had sought for it, but without finding it, they went away weeping.

'And the son of the Chan and his companion travelled onwards, and at last they came to a forest in which they found a body of Tschadkurrs quarrelling one with another, and they said, "Wherefore do ye thus quarrel one with another?"

'"I," exclaimed each of them, 'have made myself master of these boots."

'"Of what use are these boots?" inquired the son of the Chan.

'"He who wears these boots," replied the Tschadkurrs, "is conveyed to any country wherein he wishes himself."

'"Now," answered the son of the Chan, "go all of you that way, and he who first runs hither shall obtain the boots."

'And the Tschadkurrs, when they heard these words, ran as they were told; but the son of the Chan had concealed the boots in the bosom of his companion, who had the cap upon his head. And the Tschadkurrs saw the boots no more; they sought them in vain and went their way.

'And when they were gone, the prince and his companion drew on each of them one of the boots, and they wished themselves near the place of election in a Chan's kingdom. They wished their journey, laid themselves down to sleep, and on their awaking in the morning they found themselves in the hollow of a tree, right in the centre of the imperial place of election. It was, moreover, a day for the assembling of the people, to throw a Baling (a sacred figure of dough or paste) under the guidance of the Tângâri.

'"Upon whose head even the Baling falls, he shall be our Chan." Thus spoke they as they threw it up; but the tree caught the Baling of Destiny.

'"What means this?" exclaimed they all with one accord. "Shall we have a tree for our Chan?"

'"Let us examine," cried they one to another, "whether the tree conceals any stranger." And when they approached the tree, the son of the Chan and his companion stepped forth.

'But the people stood yet in doubt, and said one to another thus, "Whosoever rules over the people of this land, this shall be decided tomorrow morning by what proceeds from their mouths." And when they had thus spoken, they all took their departure.

'On the following morning, some drank water, and what they threw from their mouths was white; others ate grass, and what they threw from their mouths was green. In short, one threw one thing, and another thing. But because the son of the Chan and his companion cast out from their mouths gold and brass, the people cried, "Let the one be Chan of this people – let the other be his minister."

'Thus, were they nominated Chan and minister! And the daughter of the former Chan was appointed the wife of the new Chan.

'Now, in the neighbourhood of the palace wherein the Chan dwelt was a lofty building, whither the wife of the Chan betook herself every day. "Wherefore," thought the minister, "does the wife of the Chan betake herself to this spot every day?"

'Thus thinking, he placed the wonderful cap upon his head, and followed the Chan's wife through the open doors, up one step after another, up to the roof. Here, the wife of the Chan gathered together silken coverlets and pillows, made ready various drinks and delicate meats, and burnt for their perfume tapers and frankincense. The minister, being concealed by his cap, which made him invisible, seated himself by the side of the Chan's wife, and looked around on every side.

'Shortly afterwards, a beautiful bird swept through the sky. The wife of the Chan received it with fragrance-giving tapers. The bird seated itself upon the roof and twittered with a pleasing voice; but out of the bird came Solangdu, the Son of the Tângâri, whose beauty was incomparable, and he laid himself on the silken coverlets and fed of the dainties prepared for him.

'Then spoke the son of the Tângâri, "You have passed this morning with the husband whom your fate has allotted to you. What do you think of him?"

'The wife of the Chan answered, "I know too little of the prince to speak of his good qualities or his defects."

'Thus passed the day, and the wife of the Chan returned home again.

'On the following day, the minister followed the wife of the Chan as he had done before, and heard the son of the Tângâri say unto her, "Tomorrow I will come like a bird of Paradise to see your husband."

'And the wife of the Chan said, "Be it so."

'The day passed over, and the minister said to the Chan, "In yonder palace lives Solangdu, the beauteous son of the Tângâri."

'The minister then related all that he had witnessed, and said, "Tomorrow early, the son of the Tângâri will seek you, disguised like a bird of Paradise. I will seize the bird by the tail and cast him into the fire; but you must smite him in pieces with the sword."

'On the following morning, the Chan and the wife of the Chan were seated together, when the son of the Tângâri, transformed into a bird of Paradise, appeared before them on the steps that led to the palace. The wife of the Chan greeted the bird with looks expressive of pleasure, but the minister, who had on his invisible-making cap, seized the bird suddenly by the tail, and cast him into the fire. And the Chan smote at him violently with his sword; but the wife of the Chan seized the hand of her husband, so that only the wings of the bird were scorched. "Alas, poor bird!" exclaimed the wife of the Chan, as, half dead, it made its way, as well as it could, through the air.

'On the next morning, the wife of the Chan went as usual to the lofty building, and this time, too, did the minister follow her. She collected together, as usual, the silken pillows, but waited longer than she was wont, and sat watching with staring eyes. At length, the bird approached with a very slow flight and came down from the birdhouse covered with blood and wounds, and the wife of the Chan wept at the sight.

'"Weep not," said the son of the Tângâri; "your husband has a heavy hand. The fire has so scorched me that I can never come more."

'Thus, spoke he, and the wife of the Chan replied, "Do not say so, but come as you are wont to do, at least come on the day of the full moon."

Then the son of the Tângâri flew up to the sky again, and the wife of the Chan began from that time to love her husband with her whole heart.

'Then the minister placed his wonderful cap upon his head, and, drawing near to a pagoda he saw, through the crevice of the door, a man, who spread out a figure of an ass, rolled himself over and over upon the figure, thereupon took upon himself the form of an ass, and ran up and down braying like one. Then he began rolling afresh and appeared in his human form.

At last, he folded up the paper and placed it in the hand of a burchan (a Calmuc idol). And when the man came out, the minister went in, procured the paper, and remembering the ill-treatment which he had formerly received, he went to the mother and daughter who had sold him the strong liquor, and said, with crafty words, "I am come to you to reward you for your good deeds."

'With these words, he gave the women three pieces of gold; and the women asked him, saying, "You are, indeed, an honest man, but where did you procure so much gold?"

'Then the minister answered, "By merely rolling backwards and forwards over this paper did I procure this gold."

'On hearing these words, the women said, "Grant us that we too may roll upon it."

'And they did so and were changed into asses. And the minister brought the asses to the Chan, and the Chan said, "Let them be employed in carrying stones and earth."

'Thus spoke he, and for three years were these two asses compelled to carry stones and earth; and their backs were sore wounded, and covered with bruises. Then saw the Chan their eyes filled with tears, and he said to the minister, "Torment the poor brutes no longer."

'Thereupon they rolled upon the paper, and after they had done so they were changed to two shrivelled women.'

'Poor creatures!' exclaimed the son of the Chan.

Ssidi replied, 'Ruler of Destiny, thou hast spoken words: Ssarwala missdood jakzank!'

Thus, spoke he, and flew out of the sack through the air.

And Ssidi's second relation treats of the Adventures of the Poor Man's Son.

From: Oriental Folklore & Legends

The Charmed Ring

A MERCHANT STARTED his son in life with three hundred rupees and bade him go to another country and try his luck in trade. The son took the money and departed. He had not gone far, before he came across some herdsmen quarrelling over a dog, that some of them wished to kill.

'Please do not kill the dog,' pleaded the young and tender-hearted fellow; 'I will give you one hundred rupees for it.'

Then and there, of course, the bargain was concluded, and the foolish fellow took the dog and continued his journey. He next met with some people fighting about a cat. Some of them wanted to kill it, but others not.

'Oh! Please do not kill it,' said he; 'I will give you one hundred rupees for it.'

Of course, they at once gave him the cat and took the money. He went on till he reached a village, where some folk were quarrelling over a snake that had just been caught. Some of them wished to kill it, but others did not.

'Please do not kill the snake,' said he; 'I will give you one hundred rupees.'

Of course, the people agreed, and were highly delighted.

What a fool the fellow was! What would he do now that all his money was gone? What could he do except return to his father?

Accordingly, he went home.

'You fool! You scamp!' exclaimed his father when he had heard how his son had wasted all the money that had been given to him. 'Go and live in the stables and repent of your folly. You shall never again enter my house.'

So, the young man went and lived in the stables. His bed was the grass spread for the cattle, and his companions were the dog, the cat and the snake, which he had purchased so dearly. These creatures got very fond of him, and would follow him about during the day, and sleep by him at night; the cat used to sleep at his feet, the dog at his head, and the snake over his body, with its head hanging on one side and its tail on the other.

One day the snake in course of conversation said to its master, 'I am the son of Raja Indrasha. One day, when I had come out of the ground to drink the air, some people seized me, and would have slain me had you not most opportunely arrived to my rescue. I do not know how I shall ever be able to repay you for your great kindness to me. Would that you knew my father! How glad he would be to see his son's preserver!'

'Where does he live? I should like to see him, if possible,' said the young man.

'Well said!' continued the snake. 'Do you see yonder mountain? At the bottom of that mountain there is a sacred spring. If you will come with me and dive into that spring, we shall both reach my father's country. Oh! How glad he will be to see you! He will wish to reward you, too. But how can he do that? However, you may be pleased to accept something at his hand. If he asks you what you would like, you would, perhaps, do well to reply, "The ring on your right hand, and the famous pot and spoon which you possess."

With these in your possession, you would never need anything, for the ring is such that a man has only to speak to it, and immediately a beautiful furnished mansion will be provided for him, while the pot and the spoon will supply him with all manner of the rarest and most delicious foods.'

Attended by his three companions, the man walked to the well and prepared to jump in, according to the snake's directions.

'O master!' exclaimed the cat and dog, when they saw what he was going to do. 'What shall we do? Where shall we go?'

'Wait for me here,' he replied. 'I am not going far. I shall not be long away.'

On saying this, he dived into the water and was lost to sight.

'Now what shall we do?' said the dog to the cat.

'We must remain here,' replied the cat, 'as our master ordered. Do not be anxious about food. I will go to the people's houses and get plenty of food for both of us.'

And so, the cat did, and they both lived very comfortably till their master came again and joined them.

The young man and the snake reached their destination in safety; and information of their arrival was sent to the raja. His highness commanded his son and the stranger to appear before him. But the snake refused, saying that it could not go to its father till it was released from this stranger, who had saved it from a most terrible death, and whose slave it therefore was.

Then the raja went and embraced his son and, saluting the stranger, welcomed him to his dominions. The young man stayed there a few days, during which he received the raja's right-hand ring, and the pot and spoon, in recognition of His Highness's gratitude to him for having delivered his son. He then returned. On reaching the top of the spring, he found his friends, the dog and the cat, waiting for him. They told one another all they had experienced since they had last seen each other and were all very glad. Afterwards, they walked together to the riverside, where it was decided to try the powers of the charmed ring and pot and spoon.

The merchant's son spoke to the ring, and immediately a beautiful house and a lovely princess with golden hair appeared. He spoke to the pot and spoon, also, and the most delicious dishes of food were provided for them.

So, he married the princess, and they lived very happily for several years, until one morning the princess, while arranging her toilet, put the loose hairs into a hollow bit of reed and threw them into the river that flowed along under the window.

The reed floated on the water for many miles and was at last picked up by the prince of that country, who curiously opened it and saw the golden hair. On finding it, the prince rushed off to the palace, locked himself up in his room, and would not leave it. He had fallen desperately in love with the woman whose hair he had picked up, and refused to eat, or drink, or sleep, or move, till she was brought to him.

The king, his father, was in great distress about the matter, and did not know what to do. He feared lest his son should die and leave him without an heir. At last, he determined to seek the counsel of his aunt, who was an ogress. The old woman consented to help him, and bade him not to be anxious, as she felt certain that she would succeed in getting the beautiful woman for his son's wife.

She assumed the shape of a bee and went along buzzing, and buzzing, and buzzing. Her keen sense of smell soon brought her to the beautiful princess, to whom she appeared as an old hag, holding in one hand a stick by way of support.

She introduced herself to the beautiful princess and said, 'I am your aunt, whom you have never seen before, because I left the country just after your birth.'

She also embraced and kissed the princess by way of adding force to her words. The beautiful princess was thoroughly deceived. She returned the ogress's embrace, and invited her to come and stay in the house as long as she could, and treated her with such honour and attention, that the ogress thought to herself, 'I shall soon accomplish my errand.'

When she had been in the house three days, she began to talk of the charmed ring, and advised her to keep it instead of her husband, because the latter was constantly out shooting and on other such-like expeditions and might lose it.

Accordingly, the beautiful princess asked her husband for the ring, and he readily gave it to her.

The ogress waited another day before she asked to see the precious thing. Doubting nothing, the beautiful princess complied, when the ogress seized the ring, and reassuming the form of a bee flew away with it to the palace, where the prince was lying nearly on the point of death.

'Rise up. Be glad. Mourn no more,' she said to him. 'The woman for whom you yearn will appear at your summons. See, here is the charm, whereby you may bring her before you.'

The prince was almost mad with joy when he heard these words, and was so desirous of seeing the beautiful princess that he immediately spoke to the ring, and the house with its fair occupant descended in the midst of the palace garden.

He at once entered the building, and telling the beautiful princess of his intense love, entreated her to be his wife. Seeing no escape from the difficulty, she consented on the condition that he would wait one month for her.

Meanwhile, the merchant's son had returned from hunting and was terribly distressed not to find his house and wife. There was the place only, just as he knew it before he had tried the charmed ring which Raja Indrasha had given him. He sat down and determined to put an end to himself. Presently, the cat and dog came up. They had gone away and hidden themselves when they saw the house and everything disappear.

'O master!' they said, 'stay your hand. Your trial is great, but it can be remedied. Give us one month, and we will go and try to recover your wife and house.'

'Go,' said he, 'and may the great God aid your efforts. Bring back my wife, and I shall live.'

So, the cat and dog started off at a run and did not stop till they reached the place whither their mistress and the house had been taken.

'We may have some difficulty here,' said the cat. 'Look, the king has taken our master's wife and house for himself. You stay here. I will go to the house and try to see her.'

So, the dog sat down, and the cat climbed up to the window of the room, wherein the beautiful princess was sitting, and entered. The princess recognised the cat and informed it of all that had happened to her since she had left them. 'But is there no way of escape from the hands of these people?' she asked.

'Yes,' replied the cat, 'if you can tell me where the charmed ring is.'

'The ring is in the stomach of the ogress,' she said.

'All right,' said the cat, 'I will recover it. If we once get it, everything is ours.'

Then the cat descended the wall of the house and went and laid down by a rat's hole and pretended she was dead. Now at that time, a great wedding chanced to be going on among the rat community of that place, and all the rats of the neighbourhood were assembled in that one particular mine by which the cat had lain down. The eldest son of the king of the rats was about to be married.

The cat got to know of this, and at once conceived the idea of seizing the bridegroom and making him render the necessary help. Consequently, when the procession poured forth from the hole squealing and jumping in honour of the occasion, it immediately spotted the bridegroom and pounced down on him.

'Oh! Let me go, let me go,' cried the terrified rat.

'Oh! Let him go,' squealed all the company. 'It is his wedding day.'

'No, no,' replied the cat. 'Not unless you do something for me. Listen. The ogress, who lives in that house with the prince and his wife, has swallowed a ring, which I very much want. If you will procure it for me, I will allow the rat to depart unharmed. If you do not, then your prince dies under my feet.'

'Very well, we agree,' said they all. 'Nay, if we do not get the ring for you, devour us all.'

This was rather a bold offer. However, they accomplished the thing. At midnight, when the ogress was sound asleep, one of the rats went to her bedside, climbed up on her face, and inserted its tail into her throat; whereupon the ogress coughed violently, and the ring came out and rolled on to the floor. The rat immediately seized the precious thing and ran off with it to its king, who was very glad, and went at once to the cat and released its son.

As soon as the cat received the ring, she started back with the dog to go and tell their master the good tidings. All seemed safe now. They had only to give the ring to him, and he would speak to it, and the house and beautiful princess would again be with them, and everything would go on as happily as before.

'How glad master will be!' they thought and ran as fast as their legs could carry them. Now, on the way they had to cross a stream. The dog swam, and the cat sat on its back. Now the dog was jealous of the cat, so he asked for the ring, and threatened to throw the cat into the water if it did not give it up; whereupon the cat gave up the ring. Sorry moment, for the dog at once dropped it, and a fish swallowed it.

'Oh! What shall I do? what shall I do?' said the dog.

'What is done is done,' replied the cat. 'We must try to recover it, and if we do not succeed, we had better drown ourselves in this stream. I have a plan. You go and kill a small lamb and bring it here to me.'

'All right,' said the dog, and at once ran off. He soon came back with a dead lamb and gave it to the cat. The cat got inside the lamb and lay down, telling the dog to go away a little distance and keep quiet. Not long after this a nadhar, a bird whose look can break the bones of a fish, came and hovered over the lamb, and eventually pounced down on it to carry it away.

On this, the cat came out and jumped on to the bird, and threatened to kill it if it did not recover the lost ring. This was most readily promised by the nadhar, who immediately flew off to the king of the fishes and ordered it to make inquiries and to restore the ring. The king of the fishes did so, and the ring was found and carried back to the cat.

'Come along now; I have got the ring,' said the cat to the dog.

'No, I will not,' said the dog, 'unless you let me have the ring. I can carry it as well as you. Let me have it or I will kill you.'

So, the cat was obliged to give up the ring. The careless dog very soon dropped it again. This time it was picked up and carried off by a kite.

'See, see, there it goes – away to that big tree,' the cat exclaimed.

'Oh! Oh! What have I done?' cried the dog.

'You foolish thing, I knew it would be so,' said the cat. 'But stop your barking, or you will frighten away the bird to some place where we shall not be able to trace it.'

The cat waited till it was quite dark, and then climbed the tree, killed the kite, and recovered the ring.

'Come along,' it said to the dog when it reached the ground. 'We must make haste now. We have been delayed. Our master will die from grief and suspense. Come on.'

The dog, now thoroughly ashamed of itself, begged the cat's pardon for all the trouble it had given. It was afraid to ask for the ring the third time, so they both reached their sorrowing master in safety and gave him the precious charm.

In a moment his sorrow was turned into joy. He spoke to the ring, and his beautiful wife and house reappeared, and he and everybody were as happy as ever they could be.

From: Indian Fairy Tales

The Toad-woman

Great good luck once happened to a young woman who was living all alone in the woods with nobody near her but her little dog; for, to her surprise, she found fresh meat every morning at her door.

She was very curious to know who it was that supplied her and, watching one morning, just as the sun had risen, she saw a handsome young man gliding away into the forest. Having seen her, he became her husband, and she had a son by him.

One day, not long after this, he did not return at evening, as usual, from hunting. She waited till late at night, but he came no more.

The next day, she swung her child to sleep in its cradle, and then said to her dog, 'Take care of your brother while I am gone, and when he cries, halloo for me.'

The cradle was made of the finest wampum, and all its bandages and ornaments were of the same precious stuff.

After a short time, the woman heard the cry of the dog, and running home as fast as she could, she found her child gone, and the dog too. On looking around, she saw scattered upon the ground pieces of the wampum of her child's cradle, and she knew that the dog had been faithful, and had striven his best to save her child from being carried off, as he had been, by an old woman from a distant country called Mukakee Mindemoea, or the Toad-woman.

The mother hurried off at full speed in pursuit, and as she flew along she came, from time to time, to lodges inhabited by old women, who told her at what time the child-thief had passed; they also gave her shoes that she might follow on.

There was a number of these old women who seemed as if they were prophetesses and knew what was to come long beforehand. Each of them would say to her that when she had arrived at the next lodge, she must set the toes of the moccasins they had given her pointing homeward, and that they would return of themselves. The young woman was very careful to send back in this manner all the shoes she borrowed.

She thus followed in the pursuit, from valley to valley, and stream to stream, for many months and years; when she came at length to the lodge of the last of the friendly old grandmothers, as they were called, who gave her the last instructions how to proceed. She told her that she was near the place where her son was to be found; and she directed her to build a lodge of cedar-boughs, hard by the old Toad-woman's lodge, and to make a little bark dish, and to fill it with the juice of the wild grape.

'Then,' she said, 'your first child (meaning the dog) will come and find you out.'

These directions the young woman followed just as they had been given to her, and in a short time she heard her son, now grown up, going out to hunt, with his dog, calling out to him, 'Peewaubik – Spirit-Iron – Twee! Twee!'

The dog soon came into the lodge, and she set before him the dish of grape juice.

'See, my child,' she said, addressing him, 'the pretty drink your mother gives you.'

Spirit-Iron took a long draught, and immediately left the lodge with his eyes wide open; for it was the drink which teaches one to see the truth of things as they are. He rose up when he got into the open air, stood upon his hind legs, and looked about. 'I see how it is,' he said; and marching off, erect like a man, he sought out his young master.

Approaching him in great confidence, he bent down and whispered in his ear (having first looked cautiously around to see that no one was listening), 'This old woman here in the lodge is no mother of yours. I have found your real mother, and she is worth looking at. When we come back from our day's sport, I'll prove it to you.'

They went out into the woods, and at the close of the afternoon they brought back a great spoil of meat of all kinds. The young man, as soon as he had laid aside his weapons, said to the old Toad-woman, 'Send some of the best of this meat to the stranger who has arrived lately.'

The Toad-woman answered. 'No! Why should I send to her, the poor widow!'

The young man would not be refused; and at last, the old Toad-woman consented to take something and throw it down at the door. She called out, 'My son gives you this.'

But, being bewitched by Mukakee Mindemoea, it was so bitter and distasteful that the young woman immediately cast it out of the lodge after her.

In the evening, the young man paid the stranger a visit at her lodge of cedar-boughs. She then told him that she was his real mother, and that he had been stolen away from her by the old Toad-woman, who was a child-thief and a witch.

As the young man appeared to doubt, she added, 'Feign yourself sick when you go home to her lodge; and when the Toad-woman asks what ails you, say that you wish to see your cradle; for your cradle was of wampum, and your faithful brother the dog, in striving to save you, tore off these pieces which I show you.'

They were real wampum, white and blue, shining and beautiful; and the young man, placing them in his bosom, set off; but as he did not seem quite steady in his belief of the strange woman's story, the dog Spirit-Iron, taking his arm, kept close by his side, and gave him many words of encouragement as they went along. They entered the lodge together; and the old Toad-woman saw, from something in the dog's eye, that trouble was coming.

'Mother,' said the young man, placing his hand to his head, and leaning heavily upon Spirit-Iron, as if a sudden faintness had come upon him, 'Why am I so different in looks from the rest of your children?'

'Oh,' she answered, 'it was a very bright, clear blue sky when you were born; that is the reason.'

He seemed to be so very ill that the Toad-woman at length asked what she could do for him. He said nothing could do him good but the sight of his cradle. She ran immediately and brought a cedar cradle; but he said: 'That is not my cradle.'

She went and got another of her own children's cradles, of which there were four; but he turned his head and said: 'That is not mine; I am as sick as ever.'

When she had shown the four, and they had been all rejected, she at last produced the real cradle. The young man saw that it was of the same stuff as the wampum which he had in his bosom. He could even see the marks of the teeth of Spirit-Iron left upon the edges, where he had taken hold, striving to hold it back.

He had no doubt, now, which was his mother.

To get free of the old Toad-woman, it was necessary that the young man should kill a fat bear and, being directed by Spirit-Iron, who was very wise in such a matter, he secured the fattest in all that country; and having stripped a tall pine of all its bark and branches, he perched the carcass in the top, with its head to the east and its tail due west. Returning to the lodge, he informed the old Toad-woman that the fat bear was ready for her, but that she would have to go very far, even to the end of the earth, to get it.

She answered: 'It is not so far but that I can get it;' for of all things in the world, a fat bear was the delight of the old Toad-woman.

She at once set forth; and she was no sooner out of sight than the young man and his dog, Spirit-Iron, blowing a strong breath in the face of the Toad-woman's four children (who were all bad spirits, or bear-fiends), they put out their life. They then set them up by the side of the door, having first thrust a piece of the white fat in each of their mouths.

The Toad-woman spent a long time in finding the bear which she had been sent after, and she made at least five and twenty attempts before she was able to climb to the carcass. She slipped down three times where she went up once.

When she returned with the great bear on her back, as she drew near her lodge, she was astonished to see the four children standing up by the doorposts with the fat in their mouths. She was angry with them, and called out: 'Why do you thus insult the pomatum of your brother?'

She was still more angry when they made no answer to her complaint; but when she found that they were stark dead, and placed in this way to mock her, her fury was very great indeed. She ran after the tracks of the young man and his mother as fast as she could; so fast, indeed, that she was on the very point of overtaking them, when the dog, Spirit-Iron, coming close up to his master, whispered to him, 'Snakeberry!'

'Let the snakeberry spring up to detain her!' cried out the young man.

Immediately, the berries spread like scarlet all over the path, for a long distance; and the old Toad-woman, who was almost as fond of these berries as she was of fat bears, could not avoid stooping down to pick and eat.

The old Toad-woman was very anxious to get forward, but the snakeberry-vines kept spreading out on every side; and they still grow and grow, and spread and spread; and to this day, the wicked old Toad-woman is busy picking the berries, and she will never be able to get beyond to the other side, to disturb the happiness of the young hunter and his mother, who still live, with their faithful dog, in the shadow of the beautiful woodside where they were born.

From: The Indian Fairy Book

The King & the Juju Tree

Udo Ubok Udom was a famous king who lived at Itam, which is an inland town and does not possess a river. The king and his wife therefore used to wash at the spring just behind their house.

King Udo had a daughter, of whom he was very fond, and looked after her most carefully, and she grew up into a beautiful woman.

For some time, the king had been absent from his house, and had not been to the spring for two years. When he went to his old place to wash, he found that the Idem Juju tree had grown up all round the place, and it was impossible for him to use the spring as he had done formerly. He therefore called fifty of his young men to bring their machetes and cut down the tree. They started cutting the tree, but it had no effect as, directly they made a cut in the tree, it closed up again; so, after working all day, they found they had made no impression on it.

When they returned at night, they told the king that they had been unable to destroy the tree. He was very angry when he heard this, and went to the spring the following morning, taking his own machete with him.

When the Juju tree saw that the king had come himself and was starting to try to cut his branches, he caused a small splinter of wood to go into the king's eye. This gave the king great pain, so he threw down his machete and went back to his house. The pain, however, got worse, and he could not eat or sleep for three days.

He therefore sent for his witch men and told them to cast lots to find out why he was in such pain. When they had cast lots, they decided that the reason was that the Juju tree was angry with the king because he wanted to wash at the spring and had tried to destroy the tree.

They then told the king that he must take seven baskets of flies, a white goat, a white chicken, and a piece of white cloth, and make a sacrifice of them in order to satisfy the Juju.

The king did this, and the witch men tried their lotions on the king's eye, but it got worse and worse.

He then dismissed these witches and got another lot.

When they arrived, they told the king that, although they could do nothing themselves to relieve his pain, they knew one man who lived in the spirit land who could cure him; so, the king told them to send for him at once, and he arrived the next day.

Then the spirit man said, 'Before I do anything to your eye, what will you give me?'

So, king Udo said, 'I will give you half my town with the people in it, also seven cows and some money.'

But the spirit man refused to accept the king's offer.

As the king was in such pain, he said, 'Name your own price, and I will pay you.'

So, the spirit man said the only thing he was willing to accept as payment was the king's daughter. At this, the king cried very much and told the man to go away, as he would rather die than let him have his daughter.

That night, the pain was worse than ever, and some of his subjects pleaded with the king to send for the spirit man again and give him his daughter, and told him that when he got well he could no doubt have another daughter but that if he died now he would lose everything.

The king then sent for the spirit man again, who came very quickly, and in great grief the king handed his daughter to the spirit.

The spirit man then went out into the bush, and collected some leaves, which he soaked in water and beat up. The juice he poured into the king's eye and told him that when he washed his face in the morning, he would be able to see what was troubling him in the eye.

The king tried to persuade him to stay the night, but the spirit man refused, and departed that same night for the spirit land, taking the king's daughter with him.

Before it was light the king rose up and washed his face and found that the small splinter from the Juju tree, which had been troubling him so much, dropped out of his eye, the pain disappeared, and he was quite well again.

When he came to his proper senses, he realised that he had sacrificed his daughter for one of his eyes, so he made an order that there should be general mourning throughout his kingdom for three years.

For the first two years of the mourning the king's daughter was put in the fatting house by the spirit man and was given food. But a skull, who was in the house, told her not to eat, as they were fatting her up not for marriage, but so that they could eat her. She therefore gave all the food which was brought to her to the skull, and lived on chalk herself.

Towards the end of the third year, the spirit man brought some of his friends to see the king's daughter and told them he would kill her the next day, and they would have a good feast off her.

When she woke up in the morning, the spirit man brought her food as usual; but the skull, who wanted to preserve her life, and who had heard what the spirit man had said, called her into the room and told her what was going to happen later in the day. She handed the food to the skull, and he said, 'When the spirit man goes to the wood with his friends to prepare for the feast, you must run back to your father.'

He then gave her some medicine which would make her strong for the journey, and also gave her directions as to the road, telling her that there were two roads but that when she came to the parting of the ways she was to drop some of the medicine on the ground and the two roads would become one.

He then told her to leave by the back door and go through the wood until she came to the end of the town; she would then find the road. If she met people on the road, she was to pass them in silence, as if she saluted them, they would know that she was a stranger in the spirit land and might kill her. She was also not to turn around if anyone called to her but was to go straight on till she reached her father's house.

Having thanked the skull for his kind advice, the king's daughter started off, and when she reached the end of the town and found the road, she ran for three hours, and at last arrived at the branch roads. There, she dropped the medicine as she had been instructed, and the two roads immediately became one; so she went straight on and never saluted anyone or turned back, although several people called to her.

About this time, the spirit man had returned from the wood and went to the house, only to find the king's daughter was absent. He asked the skull where she was, and he replied that she had gone out by the back door, but he did not know where she had gone to. Being a spirit, however, he very soon guessed that she had gone home; so, he followed as quickly as possible, shouting out all the time.

When the girl heard his voice, she ran as fast as she could and at last arrived at her father's house, and told him to take at once a cow, a pig, a sheep, a goat, a dog, a chicken and seven eggs, and cut them into seven parts as a sacrifice and leave them on the road, so that when the spirit man saw these things, he would stop and not enter the town. This the king did immediately and made the sacrifice as his daughter had told him.

When the spirit man saw the sacrifice on the road, he sat down and at once began to eat. When he had satisfied his appetite, he packed up the remainder and returned to the spirit land, not troubling anymore about the king's daughter.

When the king saw that the danger was over, he beat his drum and declared that for the future, when people died and went to the spirit land, they should not come to earth again as spirits to cure sick people.

From: Folk-Stories from Southern Nigeria

The Star Lovers

All you that are true lovers, I beseech you pray the gods for fair weather upon the seventh night of the seventh moon.

For patience' sake and for dear love's sake, pray, and be pitiful that upon that night there may be neither rain, nor hail, nor cloud, nor thunder, nor creeping mist.

Hear the sad tale of the Star Lovers and give them your prayers.

The Weaving Maiden was the daughter of a Deity of Light. Her dwelling was upon the shore of the Milky Way, which is the Bright River of Heaven.

All the day long, she sat at her loom and plied her shuttle, weaving the gay garments of the gods. Warp and woof, hour by hour the coloured web grew till it lay fold on fold piled at her feet. Still, she never ceased her labour, for she was afraid. She had heard a saying: 'Sorrow, age-long sorrow, shall come upon the Weaving Maiden when she leaves her loom.'

So, she laboured, and the gods had garments to spare. But she herself, poor maiden, was ill-clad; she recked nothing of her attire or of the jewels that her father gave her. She went barefoot and let her hair hang down unconfined. Ever and anon, a long lock fell upon the loom, and back she flung it over her shoulder.

She did not play with the children of Heaven or take her pleasure with celestial youths and maidens. She did not love or weep. She was neither glad nor sorry. She sat weaving, weaving… and wove her being into the many-coloured web.

Now her father, the Deity of Light, grew angry, and said: 'Daughter, you weave too much.'

'It is my duty,' she said.

'At your age to talk of duty!' said her father. 'Out upon you!'

'Wherefore are you displeased with me, my father?' she said, and her fingers plied the shuttle.

'Are you a stock or a stone, or a pale flower by the wayside?'

'Nay,' she said, 'I am none of these.'

'Then leave your loom, my child, and live; take your pleasure, be as others are.'

'And wherefore should I be as others are?' she said.

'Never dare to question me. Come, will you leave your loom?'

She said, 'Sorrow, age-long sorrow, shall come upon the Weaving Maiden when she leaves her loom.'

'A foolish saying,' cried her father, 'not worthy of credence. What do we know of age-long sorrow? Are we not gods?'

With that, he took her shuttle from her hand gently and covered the loom with a cloth. And he caused her to be very richly attired, and they put jewels upon her and garlanded her head with flowers of Paradise. And her father gave her for spouse the Herd Boy of Heaven, who tended his flocks upon the banks of the Bright River.

Now, the Maiden was changed indeed. Her eyes were stars, and her lips were ruddy. She went dancing and singing all the day. Long hours she played with the children of Heaven, and she took her pleasure with the celestial youths and maidens. Lightly she went; her feet were shod with silver.

Her lover, the Herd Boy, held her by the hand. She laughed so that the very gods laughed with her, and High Heaven re-echoed with sounds of mirth. She was careless; little did she think of duty or of the garments of the gods. As for her loom, she never went near it from one moon's end to another.

'I have my life to live,' she said; 'I'll weave it into a web no more.'

And the Herd Boy, her lover, clasped her in his arms. Her face was all tears and smiles, and she hid it on his breast. So, she lived her life.

But her father, the Deity of Light, was angry. 'It is too much,' he said. 'Is the girl mad? She will become the laughingstock of Heaven. Besides, who is to weave the new spring garments of the gods?'

Three times he warned his daughter.

Three times she laughed softly and shook her head. 'Your hand opened the door, my father,' she said, 'but of a surety no hand either of god or of mortal can shut it.'

He said, 'You shall find it otherwise to your cost.'

And he banished the Herd Boy forever and ever to the farther side of the Bright River. The magpies flew together from far and near, and they spread their wings for a frail bridge across the river, and the Herd Boy went over by the frail bridge.

And immediately the magpies flew away to the ends of the earth and the Weaving Maiden could not follow. She was the saddest thing in Heaven. Long, long she stood upon the shore, and held out her arms to the Herd Boy, who tended his oxen desolate and in tears. Long, long she lay and wept upon the sand. Long, long she brooded, looking on the ground.

She arose and went to her loom. She cast aside the cloth that covered it. She took her shuttle in her hand.

'Age-long sorrow,' she said, 'age-long sorrow!'

Presently she dropped the shuttle. 'Ah,' she moaned, 'the pain of it,' and she leaned her head against the loom.

But in a little while she said, 'Yet I would not be as once I was. I did not love or weep, I was neither glad nor sorry. Now I love and I weep – I am glad, and I am sorry.'

Her tears fell like rain, but she took up the shuttle and laboured diligently, weaving the garments of the gods. Sometimes the web was grey with grief, sometimes it was rosy with dreams. The gods were fain to go strangely clad.

The Maiden's father, the Deity of Light, for once was well pleased. 'That is my good, diligent child,' he said. 'Now you are quiet and happy.'

'The quiet of dark despair,' she said. 'Happy! I am the saddest thing in Heaven.'

'I am sorry,' said the Deity of Light; 'what shall I do?'

'Give me back my lover.'

'Nay, child, that I cannot do. He is banished forever and ever by the decree of a Deity, that cannot be broken.'

'I knew it,' she said.

'Yet something I can do. Listen. On the seventh day of the seventh moon, I will summon the magpies together from the ends of the earth, and they shall be a bridge over the Bright River of Heaven, so that the Weaving Maiden shall lightly cross to the waiting Herd Boy on the farther shore.'

So, it was.

On the seventh day of the seventh moon came the magpies from far and near. And they spread their wings for a frail bridge. And the Weaving Maiden went over by the frail bridge. Her eyes were like stars, and her heart like a bird in her bosom. And the Herd Boy was there to meet her upon the farther shore.

And so, it is still, oh, true lovers – upon the seventh day of the seventh moon these two keep their tryst. Only if the rain falls with thunder and cloud and hail, and the Bright River of Heaven is swollen and swift, the magpies cannot make a bridge for the Weaving Maiden. Alack, the dreary time!

Therefore, true lovers, pray the gods for fair weather.

From: Green Willow & Other Japanese Fairy Tales

Childe Rowland

Childe Rowland and his brothers twain were playing at the ball, and there was their sister Burd Ellen in the midst, among them all.

Childe Rowland kicked it with his foot
And caught it with his knee;
At last, as he plunged among them all
O'er the church he made it flee.
Burd Ellen round about the aisle
To seek the ball is gone,
But long they waited, and longer still,
And she came not back again.
They sought her east; they sought her west.
They sought her up and down,
And woe were the hearts of those brethren,
For she was not to be found.

So, at last her eldest brother went to the Warlock Merlin and told him all the case, and asked him if he knew where Burd Ellen was.

'The fair Burd Ellen,' said the Warlock Merlin, 'must have been carried off by the fairies, because she went round the church 'widdershins' – the opposite way to the sun. She is now in the Dark Tower of the king of Elfland; it would take the boldest knight in Christendom to bring her back.'

'If it is possible to bring her back,' said her brother, 'I'll do it, or perish in the attempt.'

'Possible it is,' said the Warlock Merlin, 'but woe to the man or mother's son that attempts it, if he is not well taught beforehand what he is to do.'

The eldest brother of Burd Ellen was not to be put off, by any fear of danger, from attempting to get her back, so he begged the Warlock Merlin to tell him what he should do, and what he should not do, in going to seek his sister. And after he had been taught, and had repeated his lesson, he set out for Elfland.

> But long they waited, and longer still,
> With doubt and muckle pain,
> But woe were the hearts of his brethren,
> For he came not back again.

Then the second brother got tired and sick of waiting, and he went to the Warlock Merlin and asked him the same as his brother. So, he set out to find Burd Ellen.

> But long they waited, and longer still,
> With muckle doubt and pain,
> And woe were his mother's and brother's heart,
> For he came not back again.

And when they had waited and waited a good long time, Childe Rowland, the youngest of Burd Ellen's brothers, wished to go, and went to his mother, the good queen, to ask her to let him go. But she would not at first, for he was the last of her children she now had, and if he was lost, all would be lost.

But he begged, and he begged, till at last the good queen let him go, and gave him his father's good brand that never struck in vain. And as she girt it round his waist, she said the spell that would give it victory.

So, Childe Rowland said goodbye to the good queen, his mother, and went to the cave of the Warlock Merlin.

'Once more, and but once more,' he said to the Warlock, 'tell how man or mother's son may rescue Burd Ellen and her brothers twain.'

'Well, my son,' said the Warlock Merlin, 'there are but two things, simple they may seem, but hard they are to do. One thing to do, and one thing not to do. And the thing to do is this: after you have entered the land of fairy, whoever speaks to you till you meet the Burd Ellen, you must out with your father's brand and off with their head. And what you've not to do is this: bite no bit, and drink no drop, however hungry or thirsty you be; drink a drop, or bite a bit, while in Elfland you be and never will you see Middle Earth again.'

So, Childe Rowland said the two things over and over again, till he knew them by heart, and he thanked the Warlock Merlin and went on his way. And he went along, and along, and along, and still further along, till he came to the horseherd of the king of Elfland feeding his horses.

These he knew by their fiery eyes and knew that he was at last in the land of Fairy.

'Can you tell me,' said Childe Rowland to the horse-herd, 'where the king of Elfland's Dark Tower is?'

'I cannot tell you,' said the horseherd, 'but go on a little further and you will come to the cowherd, and he, maybe, can tell you.'

Then, without a word more, Childe Rowland drew the good brand that never struck in vain, and off went the horseherd's head, and Childe Rowland went on further, till he came to the cowherd, and asked him the same question.

'I can't tell thee,' said he, 'but go on a little farther, and thou wilt come to the hen-wife, and she is sure to know.'

Then Childe Rowland, out with his good brand that never struck in vain, and off went the cowherd's head. And he went on a little further, till he came to an old woman in a grey cloak, and he asked her if she knew where the Dark Tower of the king of Elfland was.

'Go on a, little further,' said the henwife, 'till you come to a round green hill, surrounded with terrace-rings, from the bottom to the top; go round it three times, widdershins, and each time say:

> Open, door! open, door!
> And let me come in…

'And the third time the door will open, and you may go in.'

And Childe Rowland was just going on, when he remembered what he had to do; so, he out with the good brand that never struck in vain, and off went the henwife's head.

Then he went on, and on, and on, till he came to the round green hill with the terrace-rings from top to bottom, and he went round it three times, widdershins, saying each time:

> 'Open, door! open, door!
> And let me come in.'

And the third time, the door did open, and he went in and it closed with a click, and Childe Rowland was left in the dark.

It was not exactly dark, but a kind of twilight or gloaming. There were neither windows nor candles, and he could not make out where the twilight came from, if not through the walls and roof. These were rough arches made of a transparent rock, incrusted with sheep silver and rock spar, and other bright stones.

But though it was rock, the air was quite warm, as it always is in Elfland. So, he went through this passage till at last he came to two wide and high folding-doors which stood ajar. And when he opened them, there he saw a most wonderful and glorious sight. A large and spacious hall, so large that it seemed to be as long, and as broad, as the green hill itself. The roof was supported by fine pillars, so large and lofty, that the pillars of a cathedral were as nothing to them.

They were all of gold and silver, with fretted work, and between them and around them, wreaths of flowers, composed of what do you think? Why, of diamonds and emeralds, and all manner of precious stones. And the very keystones of the arches had for ornaments clusters of diamonds and rubies, and pearls, and other precious stones. And all these arches met in the middle of the roof, and just there, hung by a gold chain, an immense lamp made out of one big pearl hollowed out and quite transparent. And in the middle of this was a big, huge carbuncle, which kept spinning round and round, and this was what gave light by its rays to the whole hall, which seemed as if the setting sun was shining on it.

The hall was furnished in a manner equally grand, and at one end of it was a glorious couch of velvet, silk and gold, and there sat Burd Ellen, combing her golden hair with a silver comb. And when she saw Childe Rowland she stood up and said:

'God pity ye, poor luckless fool,
What have ye here to do?
'Hear ye this, my youngest brother,
Why didn't ye bide at home?
Had you a hundred thousand lives
Ye couldn't spare any a one.
'But sit ye down; but woe, O, woe,
That ever ye were born,
For come the king of Elfland in,
Your fortune is forlorn.'

Then they sat down together, and Childe Rowland told her all that he had done, and she told him how their two brothers had reached the Dark Tower, but had been enchanted by the king of Elfland and lay there entombed as if dead.

And then after they had talked a little longer, Childe Rowland began to feel hungry from his long travels and told his sister Burd Ellen how hungry he was and asked for some food, forgetting all about the Warlock Merlin's warning.

Burd Ellen looked at Childe Rowland sadly, and shook her head, but she was under a spell, and could not warn him. So, she rose up, and went out, and soon brought back a golden basin full of bread and milk. Childe Rowland was just going to raise it to his lips, when he looked at his sister and remembered why he had come all that way. So, he dashed the bowl to the ground, and said: 'Not a sup will I swallow, nor a bit will I bite, till Burd Ellen is set free.'

Just at that moment they heard the noise of someone approaching, and a loud voice was heard saying:

'Fee, fi, fo, fum,
I smell the blood of a Christian man,
Be he dead, be he living, with my brand,
I'll dash his brains from his brain-pan.'

And then, the folding-doors of the hall were burst open, and the king of Elfland rushed in.

'Strike then, Bogle, if you dare,' shouted out Childe Rowland, and rushed to meet him with his good brand that never yet did fail. They fought, and they fought, and they fought, till Childe Rowland beat the king of Elfland down on to his knees and caused him to yield and beg for mercy.

'I grant you mercy,' said Childe Rowland, 'release my sister from your spells and raise my brothers to life, and let us all go free, and you shall be spared.'

'I agree,' said the Elfin king and, rising up, he went to a chest from which he took a phial filled with a blood-red liquor.

With this, he anointed the ears, eyelids, nostrils, lips, and fingertips, of the two brothers, and they sprang at once into life, and declared that their souls had been away, but had now returned.

The Elfin king then said some words to Burd Ellen, and she was disenchanted, and they all four passed out of the hall, through the long passage, and turned their back on the Dark Tower, never to return again.

And they reached home, and the good queen, their mother, and Burd Ellen never went round a church widdershins again.

From: English Fairy Tales

The Cobbler of Burgos

Not far from the Garden of the Widows in Burgos lived a cobbler who was so poor that he had not even smiled for many years.

Every day, he saw the widow ladies pass his small shop on the way to and from the garden; but in their bereavement it would not have been considered correct for them to have bestowed a glance on him, and they required all the money they could scrape together, after making ample provision for their comfort – which, as ladies, they did not neglect – to pay for Masses for the repose of the souls of their husbands, according to the doctrines of the faith which was pinned on to them in childhood.

The priests, however, would sometimes bestow their blessing on Sancho the cobbler; but beyond words, he got nothing from the comforters of the widows and of the orphans.

Some of the great families would have their boots soled by him; but being very great and rich people, they demanded long credit, so that he was heard to say that a rich man's money was almost as scarce as virtue.

Now, one night, when he was about to close his shop, a lovely young widow lady pushed her way by him into the shop, and sitting on the only chair in the room, she bid him close the door immediately, as she had something to say to him in confidence.

Being a true Spaniard, he showed no surprise, but obeyed orders, and stood before the young widow lady who, after looking at him carefully for a minute, implored him to go upstairs and see that the windows were secure, and the shutters barred and bolted.

This done, he again stood before her, when she showed signs of fear, and requested him to ensure against the doors being burst open by piling what furniture he had against them and against the shutters; and then, assuring herself that she was safe, she exclaimed – 'Ah, friend Sancho, it is good to beware of evil tongues. I come to you because I know you to be honest and silent. Tonight, you must sleep on the roof; get out through the skylight, and I will rest here.'

To refuse a lady's commands, however singular they may be, is not in the nature of a Spaniard, so Sancho got out through the skylight, when the young widow began screaming, 'Let me out, kind people – let me out!'

The cobbler was now very much afraid of the consequences, especially as the night watchmen were banging against the street door, which they soon forced, knocking all the furniture which had been placed against it into the middle of the room.

When inside, they discovered the lovely young widow, who exclaimed, 'Good men, I am Guiomar, of Torrezon, widow of the noble Pedro de Torrezon, and because my late husband was owing Sancho for soling a pair of boots, I came here to pay the debt; but Sancho would have detained me against my will. He is concealed on the roof of the house, and if you leave me here, he will murder me.'

Then she naturally fainted and screamed for so long a time that the street was soon full of people who, hearing what had happened, cried out against Sancho.

The watchmen having secured him, he was led before the alcaide, and, being a poor man, he was sent to prison until such time as Doña Guiomar should feel disposed to pardon him.

At the end of a year, Doña Guiomar obtained his liberty, but on the condition that he should forthwith proceed to Rome and do penance, which was to count for the benefit of her deceased husband.

This act of piety on her part was very much approved of by the priests, who required of Sancho that during the whole of his pilgrimage there he should not shave, nor have his hair nor his nails cut. He was, furthermore, to wear a suit of horsehair cloth next to his skin, and was to subsist solely on onions, garlic, maize bread, and pure water.

But liberty is so sweet that Sancho did not mind his hard fare, and he went on his way to Rome repeating penitential prayers, while his hair and beard grew until his head and face were nearly hidden.

Arrived at Rome, the people wondered much to see such a strange-looking being; but when he opened his mouth to inquire his way to St. Peter's, so strong was the smell of onions and garlic that the people, accustomed as they were to these vegetables, could not stand against it, and as Sancho spoke in a foreign tongue they could not have understood him very easily.

At last, he met a priest who was kind enough to listen to him, and he said he would be allowed audience of the Pope next morning with other pilgrims, but that meantime he had better confess what his fault had been.

Sancho recounted all about the lovely young widow, and the priest very properly admonished him for having dared to frighten a lady whose anxiety respecting her deceased husband was quite enough of sorrow without having it added to by being forcibly detained by a cobbler.

'It is a pity,' said the worthy priest, 'that you were not handed over to the inquisitorial brothers, for they would have burned you before you were allowed to import the odour of all the fields of Spanish onions and garlic into the Eternal City. It is a sign of the bad times that are approaching when errant cobblers are allowed to vitiate the precincts of St. Peter's with their pestilential breath. Tomorrow you will be regaled with a view – mind, only a view – of his holiness's toe, and then you must depart this city.'

Sancho recognized the truth of what the good priest said, and, having refreshed himself with some more onions and a glass of water, he lay down to sleep behind one of the large stone pillars and slept until next morning, when the large bell of the cathedral awoke him. He then hurried into the presence of the Pope, nor had he much difficulty in so doing, for the other pilgrims were glad to get out of his way. Bowing low before the golden chair, he exclaimed,

'One weary soul, though cobbler he by trade,
Comes here to seek a pardon for his sin;
Most holy father, ere the daylight fade,
Oh, let me in!
'From sunny Spain, where runs the Arlanzon,

To thee, oh, father, come I now to crave
That thou wilt raise Don Pedro Torrezon
From restless grave,
'And to his widow him restore again.
This done, dismiss me to my home in peace,
To be thy servant as a priest in Spain,
And faith increase.'

To which the Pope replied,

'We smelt thee from afar, oh, son of Spain;
We know thy errand, and we grant thy prayer.
Where onions shed their perfume, son, remain,
Thy presence spare.
'Yes, spare us all thy Spanish odours strong;
Return unto thy country, Sancho – go;
And as a blessing on thy journey long,
Stoop, kiss our toe.'

And when Sancho got back to Burgos, he was met by Don Pedro de Torrezon, who, half in anger and half in sorrow, exclaimed,

'Good Sancho, I would spend eternity
Surrounded by the pains of purgat'ry,
Than be restored unto this mortal life,
Where purgat'ry is but the name for wife.'

From: Tales from the Lands of Nuts & Grapes

The Weaver's Son & the Giant of the White Hill

THERE WAS ONCE a weaver in Erin who lived at the edge of a wood; and on a time when he had nothing to burn, he went out with his daughter to get fagots for the fire.

They gathered two bundles and were ready to carry them home, when who should come along but a splendid looking stranger on horseback. And he said to the weaver: 'My good man, will you give me that girl of yours?'

'Indeed, then I will not,' said the weaver.

'I'll give you her weight in gold,' said the stranger, and he put out the gold there on the ground.

So, the weaver went home with the gold and without the daughter. He buried the gold in the garden, without letting his wife know what he had done.

When she asked, 'Where is our daughter?'

The weaver said: 'I sent her on an errand to a neighbour's house for things that I want.'

Night came, but no sight of the girl. The next time he went for fagots, the weaver took his second daughter to the wood; and when they had two bundles gathered and were ready to go home, a second stranger came on horseback, much finer than the first, and asked the weaver would he give him his daughter.

'I will not,' said the weaver.

'Well,' said the stranger, 'I'll give you her weight in silver if you'll let her go with me;' and he put the silver down before him.

The weaver carried home the silver and buried it in the garden with the gold, and the daughter went away with the man on horseback.

When he went again to the wood, the weaver took his third daughter with him; and when they were ready to go home, a third man came on horseback, gave the weight of the third daughter in copper, and took her away. The weaver buried the copper with the gold and silver.

Now, the wife was lamenting and moaning night and day for her three daughters and gave the weaver no rest till he told the whole story.

Now, a son was born to them; and when the boy grew up and was going to school, he heard how his three sisters had been carried away for their weight in gold and silver and copper; and every day when he came home he saw how his mother was lamenting and wandering outside in grief through the fields and pits and ditches, so he asked her what trouble was on her; but she wouldn't tell him a word.

At last, he came home crying from school one day, and said: 'I'll not sleep three nights in one house till I find my three sisters.'

Then he said to his mother: 'Make me three loaves of bread, mother, for I am going on a journey.'

Next day, he asked had she the bread ready. She said she had, and she was crying bitterly all the time.

'I'm going to leave you now, mother,' said he; 'and I'll come back when I have found my three sisters.'

He went away, and walked on till he was tired and hungry; and then he sat down to eat the bread that his mother had given him, when a red-haired man came up and asked him for something to eat.

'Sit down here,' said the boy. He sat down, and the two ate till there was not a crumb of the bread left.

The boy told of the journey he was on; then the red-haired man said: 'There may not be much use in your going, but here are three things that'll serve you, – the sword of sharpness, the cloth of plenty, and the cloak of darkness. No man can kill you while that sword is in your hand; and whenever you are hungry or dry, all you have to do is to spread the cloth and ask for what you'd like to eat or drink, and it will be there before you.

When you put on the cloak, there won't be a man or a woman or a living thing in the world that'll see you, and you'll go to whatever place you have set your mind on quicker than any wind.'

The red-haired man went his way, and the boy travelled on. Before evening, a great shower came, and he ran for shelter to a large oak-tree. When he got near the tree, his foot slipped, the ground opened, and down he went through the earth till he came to another country.

When he was in the other country, he put on the cloak of darkness and went ahead like a blast of wind, and never stopped till he saw a castle in the distance; and soon he was there. But he found nine gates closed before him, and no way to go through. It was written inside the cloak of darkness that his eldest sister lived in that castle.

He was not long at the gate looking in when a girl came to him and said, 'Go on out of that; if you don't, you'll be killed.'

'Do you go in,' said he to the girl, 'and tell my sister, the woman of this castle, to come out to me.'

The girl ran in; out came the sister, and asked: 'Why are you here, and what did you come for?'

'I have come to this country to find my three sisters, who were given away by my father for their weight in gold, silver, and copper; and you are my eldest sister.'

She knew from what he said that he was her brother, so she opened the gates and brought him in, saying: 'Don't wonder at anything you see in this castle. My husband is enchanted. I see him only at night. He goes off every morning, stays away all day, and comes home in the evening.'

The sun went down; and while they were talking, the husband rushed in, and the noise of him was terrible. He came in the form of a ram, ran upstairs, and soon after came down a man.

'Who is this that's with you?' asked he of the wife.

'Oh! that's my brother, who has come from Erin to see me,' said she.

Next morning, when the man of the castle was going off in the form of a ram, he turned to the boy and asked, 'Will you stay a few days in my castle? You are welcome.'

'Nothing would please me better,' said the boy; 'but I have made a vow never to sleep three nights in one house till I have found my three sisters.'

'Well,' said the ram, 'since you must go, here is something for you.'

And, pulling out a bit of his own wool, he gave it to the boy, saying: 'Keep this; and whenever a trouble is on you, take it out, and call on what rams are in the world to help you.'

Away went the ram. The boy took farewell of his sister, put on the cloak of darkness, and disappeared. He travelled till hungry and tired, then he sat down, took off the cloak of darkness, spread the cloth of plenty, and asked for meat and drink. After he had eaten and drunk his fill, he took up the cloth, put on the cloak of darkness, and went ahead, passing every wind that was before him, and leaving every wind that was behind.

About an hour before sunset, he saw the castle in which his second sister lived. When he reached the gate, a girl came out to him and said: 'Go away from that gate, or you'll be killed.'

'I'll not leave this till my sister who lives in the castle comes out and speaks to me.'

The girl ran in, and out came the sister. When she heard his story and his father's name, she knew that he was her brother, and said: 'Come into the castle but think nothing of what you'll see or hear. I don't see my husband from morning till night. He goes and comes in a strange form, but he is a man at night.'

About sunset there was a terrible noise, and in rushed the man of the castle in the form of a tremendous salmon. He went flapping upstairs; but he wasn't long there till he came down a fine-looking man.

'Who is that with you?' asked he of the wife. 'I thought you would let no one into the castle while I was gone.'

'Oh! This is my brother, who has come to see me,' said she.

'If he's your brother, he's welcome,' said the man.

They supped, and then slept till morning. When the man of the castle was going out again, in the form of a great salmon, he turned to the boy and said: 'You'd better stay here with us a while.'

'I cannot,' said the boy. 'I made a vow never to sleep three nights in one house till I had seen my three sisters. I must go on now and find my third sister.'

The salmon then took off a piece of his fin and gave it to the boy, saying: 'If any difficulty meets you, or trouble comes on you, call on what salmons are in the sea to come and help you.'

They parted. The boy put on his cloak of darkness, and away he went, more swiftly than any wind. He never stopped till he was hungry and thirsty. Then he sat down, took off his cloak of darkness, spread the cloth of plenty, and ate his fill; when he had eaten, he went on again till near sundown, when he saw the castle where his third sister lived. All three castles were near the sea. Neither sister knew what place she was in, and neither knew where the other two were living.

The third sister took her brother in just as the first and second had done, telling him not to wonder at anything he saw.

They were not long inside when a roaring noise was heard, and in came the greatest eagle that ever was seen. The eagle hurried upstairs, and soon came down a man.

'Who is that stranger there with you?' asked he of the wife. (He, as well as the ram and salmon, knew the boy; he only wanted to try his wife.)

'This is my brother, who has come to see me.'

They all took supper and slept that night. When the eagle was going away in the morning, he pulled a feather out of his wing, and said to the boy: 'Keep this; it may serve you. If you are ever in straits and want help, call on what eagles are in the world, and they'll come to you.'

There was no hurry now, for the third sister was found; and the boy went upstairs with her to examine the country all around, and to look at the sea. Soon, he saw a great white hill, and on the top of the hill a castle.

'In that castle on the white hill beyond,' said the sister, 'lives a giant, who stole from her home the most beautiful young woman in the world. From all parts, the greatest heroes and champions and kings' sons are coming to take her away from the giant and marry her. There is not a man of them all who is able to conquer the giant and free the young woman; but the giant conquers them, cuts their heads off, and then eats their flesh. When he has picked the bones clean, he throws them out; and the whole place around the castle is white with the bones of the men that the giant has eaten.'

'I must go,' said the boy, 'to that castle to know can I kill the giant and bring away the young woman.'

So, he took leave of his sister, put on the cloak of darkness, took his sword with him, and was soon inside the castle. The giant was fighting with champions outside. When the boy saw the young woman, he took off the cloak of darkness and spoke to her.

'Oh!' said she, 'what can you do against the giant? No man has ever come to this castle without losing his life. The giant kills every man; and no one has ever come here so big that the giant did not eat him at one meal.'

'And is there no way to kill him?' asked the boy.

'I think not,' said she.

'Well, if you'll give me something to eat, I'll stay here; and when the giant comes in, I'll do my best to kill him. But don't let on that I am here.'

Then he put on the cloak of darkness, and no one could see him. When the giant came in, he had the bodies of two men on his back. He threw down the bodies and told the young woman to get them ready for his dinner. Then he snuffed around, and said: 'There's someone here; I smell the blood of an Erineach.'

'I don't think you do,' said the young woman; 'I can't see anyone.'

'Neither can I,' said the giant; 'but I smell a man.'

With that, the boy drew his sword; and when the giant was struck, he ran in the direction of the blow to give one back; then he was struck on the other side.

They were at one another this way, the giant and the boy with the cloak of darkness on him, till the giant had fifty wounds, and was covered with blood. Every minute, he was getting a slash of a sword, but never could give one back.

At last, he called out: 'Whoever you are, wait till tomorrow, and I'll face you then.'

So, the fighting stopped; and the young woman began to cry and lament as if her heart would break when she saw the state the giant was in.

'Oh! You'll be with me no longer; you'll be killed now: what can I do alone without you?' and she tried to please him, and washed his wounds.

'Don't be afraid,' said the giant; 'this one, whoever he is, will not kill me, for there is no man in the world that can kill me.'

Then the giant went to bed and was well in the morning.

Next day, the giant and the boy began in the middle of the forenoon, and fought till the middle of the afternoon. The giant was covered with wounds, and he had not given one blow to the boy, and could not see him, for he was always in his cloak of darkness. So, the giant had to ask for rest till next morning.

While the young woman was washing and dressing the wounds of the giant she cried and lamented all the time, saying: 'What'll become of me now? I'm afraid you'll be killed this time; and how can I live here without you?'

'Have no fear for me,' said the giant; 'I'll put your mind at rest. In the bottom of the sea is a chest locked and bound, in that chest is a duck, in the duck an egg; and I never can be killed unless someone gets the egg from the duck in the chest at the bottom of the sea and rubs it on the mole that is under my right breast.'

While the giant was telling this to the woman to put her mind at rest, who should be listening to the story but the boy in the cloak of darkness. The minute he heard of the chest in the sea, he thought of the salmons. So off he hurried to the seashore, which was not far away. Then, he took out the fin that his eldest sister's husband had given him, and called on what salmons were in the sea to bring up the chest with the duck inside, and put it out on the beach before him.

He had not long to wait till he saw nothing but salmo – the whole sea was covered with them, moving to land, and they put the chest out on the beach before him.

But the chest was locked and strong; how could he open it? He thought of the rams; and taking out the lock of wool, said: 'I want what rams are in the world to come and break open this chest!'

That minute the rams of the world were running to the seashore, each with a terrible pair of horns on him; and soon they battered the chest to splinters. Out flew the duck, and away she went over the sea.

The boy took out the feather, and said: 'I want what eagles are in the world to get me the egg from that duck.'

That minute, the duck was surrounded by the eagles of the world, and the egg was soon brought to the boy. He put the feather, the wool, and the fin in his pocket, put on the cloak of darkness, and went to the castle on the white hill, and told the young woman, when she was dressing the wounds of the giant again, to raise up his arm.

Next day, they fought till the middle of the afternoon. The giant was almost cut to pieces and called for a cessation.

The young woman hurried to dress the wounds, and he said: 'I see you would help me if you could: you are not able. But never fear, I shall not be killed.'

Then she raised his arm to wash away the blood, and the boy, who was there in his cloak of darkness, struck the mole with the egg. The giant died that minute.

The boy took the young woman to the castle of his third sister. Next day, he went back for the treasures of the giant, and there was more gold in the castle than one horse could draw.

They spent nine days in the castle of the eagle with the third sister. Then the boy gave back the feather, and the two went on till they came to the castle of the salmon, where they spent nine more days with the second sister; and he gave back the fin.

When they came to the castle of the ram, they spent fifteen days with the first sister, and had great feasting and enjoyment. Then the boy gave back the lock of wool to the ram, and taking farewell of his sister and her husband, set out for home with the young woman of the white castle, who was now his wife, bringing presents from the three daughters to their father and mother.

At last, they reached the opening near the tree, came up through the ground, and went on to where he met the red-haired man. Then he spread the cloth of plenty, asked for every good meat and drink, and called the red-haired man. He came. The three sat down and ate and drank with enjoyment.

When they had finished, the boy gave back to the red-haired man the cloak of darkness, the sword of sharpness, and the cloth of plenty, and thanked him.

'You were kind to me,' said the red-haired man; 'you gave me of your bread when I asked for it and told me where you were going. I took pity on you; for I knew you never could get what you wanted unless I helped you. I am the brother of the eagle, the salmon, and the ram.'

They parted. The boy went home, built a castle with the treasure of the giant, and lived happily with his parents and wife.

From: Myths and Folklore of Ireland

The Plant of Life

When he had saluted the Cat respectfully, Henry ran towards the garden of the plant of life, which was only a hundred steps from him. He trembled, lest some new obstacle should retard him, but he reached the garden lattice without any difficulty. He sought the gate and found it readily, as the garden was not large.

But alas! The garden was filled with innumerable plants utterly unknown to him and it was impossible to know how to distinguish the plant of life. Happily, he remembered that the good fairy Bienfaisante had told him that when he reached the summit of the mountain, he must call the doctor who cultivated the garden of the fairies. He called him then with a loud voice.

In a moment, he heard a noise among the plants near him and saw issue from them a little man, no taller than a hearth brush. He had a book under his arm, spectacles on his crooked little nose and wore the great black cloak of a doctor.

'What are you seeking, little one?' said the doctor; 'and how is it possible that you have gained this summit?'

'Doctor, I come from the fairy Bienfaisante to ask the plant of life to cure my poor sick mother, who is about to die.'

'All those who come from the fairy Bienfaisante,' said the little doctor, raising his hat respectfully, 'are most welcome. Come, my boy, I will give you the plant you seek.'

The doctor then buried himself in the botanical garden where Henry had some trouble in following him, as he was so small as to disappear entirely among the plants. At last, they arrived near a bush growing by itself. The doctor drew a little pruning-knife from his pocket, cut a bunch and gave it to Henry, saying: 'Take this and use it as the good fairy Bienfaisante directed but do not allow it to leave your hands. If you lay it down under any circumstances, it will escape from you and you will never recover it.'

Henry was about to thank him, but the little man had disappeared in the midst of his medicinal herbs, and he found himself alone.

'What shall I do now in order to arrive quickly at home? If I encounter on my return the same obstacles which met me as I came up the mountain, I shall perhaps lose my plant, my dear plant, which should restore my dear mother to life.'

Happily, Henry now remembered the stick which the Wolf had given him. 'Well, let us see,' said he, 'if this stick has really the power to carry me home.'

Saying this, he mounted the stick and wished himself at home. In the same moment, he felt himself raised in the air, through which he passed with the rapidity of lightning and found himself almost instantly by his mother's bed.

Henry sprang to his mother and embraced her tenderly. But she neither saw nor heard him. He lost no time but pressed the plant of life upon her lips. At the same moment she opened her eyes, threw her arms around Henry's neck and exclaimed: 'My child! My dear Henry! I have been very sick but now I feel almost well. I am hungry.'

Then, looking at him in amazement, she said: 'How you have grown, my darling! How is this? How can you have changed so in a few days?'

Henry had indeed grown a head taller. Two years, seven months and six days had passed away since he left his home. He was now nearly ten years old. Before he had time to answer, the window opened, and the good fairy Bienfaisante appeared. She embraced Henry and, approaching the couch of his mother, related to her all that little Henry had done and suffered, the dangers he had dared, the fatigues he endured; the courage, the patience, the goodness he had manifested. Henry blushed on hearing himself thus praised by the fairy. His mother pressed him to her heart and covered him with kisses.

After the first moments of happiness and emotion had passed away, the fairy said: 'Now, Henry, you can make use of the present of the little Old Man and the Giant of the mountain.'

Henry drew out his little box and opened it. Immediately, there issued from it a crowd of little workmen, not larger than bees, who filled the room. They began to work with such promptitude that in a quarter of an hour they had built and furnished a beautiful house in the midst of a lovely garden with a thick wood on one side and a beautiful meadow on the other.

'All this is yours, my brave Henry,' said the fairy. 'The Giant's thistle will obtain for you all that is necessary. The Wolf's staff will transport you where you wish. The Cat's claw will preserve your health and your youth and also that of your dear mother. Adieu, Henry! Be happy and never forget that virtue and filial love are always recompensed.'

Henry threw himself on his knees before the fairy, who gave him her hand to kiss, smiled upon him and disappeared.

Henry's mother had a great desire to arise from her bed and admire her new house, her garden, her woods and her meadow. But alas! she had no dress. During her first illness she had made Henry sell all that she possessed, as they were suffering for bread.

'Alas! Alas! My child, I cannot leave my bed. I have neither dresses nor shoes.'

'You shall have all those things, dear mother,' exclaimed Henry.

Drawing his thistle from his pocket, he smelled it while he wished for dresses, linen, shoes for his mother and himself and also for linen for the house.

At the same moment, the presses were filled with linen, his mother was dressed in a good and beautiful robe of merino and Henry completely clothed in blue cloth, with good, substantial shoes. They both uttered a cry of joy. His mother sprang from her bed to run through the house with Henry. Nothing was wanting. Everywhere, the furniture was good and comfortable. The kitchen was filled with pots and kettles; but there was nothing in them.

Henry again put his thistle to his nose and desired to have a good dinner served up.

A table soon appeared, with good smoking soup, a splendid leg of lamb, a roasted pullet and good salad. They took seats at the table with the appetite of those who had not eaten for three years. The soup was soon swallowed, the leg of lamb entirely eaten, then the pullet, then the salad.

When their hunger was thus appeased the mother, aided by Henry, took off the cloth, washed and arranged all the dishes and then put the kitchen in perfect order. They then made up their beds with the sheets they found in the presses and went happily to bed, thanking God and the good fairy Bienfaisante. The mother also gave grateful thanks for her dear son Henry.

They lived thus most happily; they wanted nothing – the thistle provided everything. They did not grow old or sick – the claw cured every ill. They never used the staff, as they were too happy at home ever to desire to leave it.

Henry asked of his thistle only two cows, two good horses and the necessaries of life for every day. He wished for nothing superfluous, either in clothing or food and thus he preserved his thistle as long as he lived.

It is not known when they died. It is supposed that the queen of the fairies made them immortal and transported them to her palace, where they still are.

From: Old French Fairy Tales

The Werewolf

Once upon a time, there was a king who reigned over a great kingdom.

He had a queen, but only a single daughter, a girl. In consequence, the little girl was the apple of her parents' eyes; they loved her above everything else in the world, and their dearest thought was the pleasure they would take in her when she was older. But the unexpected often happens; for before the king's daughter began to grow up, the queen her mother fell ill and died.

It is not hard to imagine the grief that reigned, not alone in the royal castle, but throughout the land; for the queen had been beloved of all. The king grieved so that he would not marry again, and his one joy was the little princess.

A long time passed, and with each succeeding day, the king's daughter grew taller and more beautiful, and her father granted her every wish. Now, there were a number of women who had nothing to do but wait on the princess and carry out her commands. Among them was a woman who had formerly married and had two daughters.

She had an engaging appearance, a smooth tongue and a winning way of talking, and she was as soft and pliable as silk; but at heart she was full of machinations and falseness.

Now, when the queen died, she at once began to plan how she might marry the king, so that her daughters might be kept like royal princesses.

With this end in view, she drew the young princess to her, paid her the most fulsome compliments on everything she said and did, and was forever bringing the conversation around to how happy she would be were the king to take another wife.

There was much said on this head, early and late, and before very long the princess came to believe that the woman knew all there was to know about everything. So, she asked her what sort of a woman the king ought to choose for a wife.

The woman answered as sweet as honey: 'It is not my affair to give advice in this matter; yet he should choose for queen someone who is kind to the little princess. For one thing I know, and that is, were I fortunate enough to be chosen, my one thought would be to do all I could for the little princess, and if she wished to wash her hands, one of my daughters would have to hold the washbowl and the other hand her the towel.'

This and much more she told the king's daughter, and the princess believed it, as children will.

From that day forward, the princess gave her father no peace and begged him again and again to marry the good court lady. Yet he did not want to marry her. But the king's daughter gave him no rest; but urged him again and again, as the false court lady had persuaded her to do. Finally, one day, when she again brought up the matter, the king cried: 'I can see you will end by having your own way about this, even though it be entirely against my will. But I will do so only on one condition.'

'What is the condition?' asked the princess.

'If I marry again,' said the king, 'it is only because of your ceaseless pleading. Therefore, you must promise that, if in the future you are not satisfied with your stepmother or your stepsisters, not a single lament or complaint on your part reaches my ears.'

This she promised the king, and it was agreed that he should marry the court lady and make her queen of the whole country.

As time passed on, the king's daughter had grown to be the most beautiful maiden to be found far and wide; the queen's daughters, on the other hand, were homely, evil of disposition, and no one knew any good of them.

Hence it was not surprising that many youths came from East and West to sue for the princess's hand; but that none of them took any interest in the queen's daughters. This made the stepmother very angry; but she concealed her rage and was as sweet and friendly as ever.

Among the wooers was a king's son from another country. He was young and brave, and since he loved the princess dearly, she accepted his proposal, and they plighted their troth. The queen observed this with an angry eye, for it would have pleased her had the prince chosen one of her own daughters. She therefore made up her mind that the young pair should never be happy together, and from that time on thought only of how she might part them from each other.

An opportunity soon offered itself.

News came that the enemy had entered the land, and the king was compelled to go to war. Now the princess began to find out the kind of stepmother she had. For no sooner had the king departed, than the queen showed her true nature and was just as harsh and unkind as she formerly had pretended to be friendly and obliging.

Not a day went by without her scolding and threatening the princess; and the queen's daughters were every bit as malicious as their mother. But the king's son, the lover of the princess, found himself in even worse position.

He had gone hunting one day, had lost his way, and could not find his people. Then the queen used her black arts and turned him into a werewolf, to wander through the forest for the remainder of his life in that shape.

When evening came and there was no sign of the prince, his people returned home, and one can imagine what sorrow they caused when the princess learned how the hunt had ended. She grieved, wept day and night, and was not to be consoled. But the queen laughed at her grief, and her heart was filled with joy to think that all had turned out exactly as she wished.

Now it chanced one day, as the king's daughter was sitting alone in her room, that she thought she would go herself into the forest where the prince had disappeared. She went to her stepmother and begged permission to go out into the forest, in order to forget her surpassing grief. The queen did not want to grant her request, for she always preferred saying no to yes. But the princess begged her so winningly that at last she was unable to say no, and she ordered one of her daughters to go along with her and watch her.

That caused a great deal of discussion, for neither of the stepdaughters wanted to go with her; each made all sorts of excuses, and asked what pleasures were there in going with the king's daughter, who did nothing but cry. But the queen had the last word in the end and ordered that one of her daughters must accompany the princess, even though it be against her will.

So, the girls wandered out of the castle into the forest. The king's daughter walked among the trees, and listened to the song of the birds, and thought of her lover, for whom she longed, and who was now no longer there. And the queen's daughter followed her, vexed, in her malice, with the king's daughter and her sorrow.

After they had walked a while, they came to a little hut, lying deep in the dark forest. By then the king's daughter was very thirsty and wanted to go into the little hut with her stepsister, in order to get a drink of water.

But the queen's daughter was much annoyed and said: 'Is it not enough for me to be running around here in the wilderness with you? Now you even want me, who am a princess, to enter that wretched little hut. No, I will not step a foot over the threshold! If you want to go in, why go in alone!'

The king's daughter lost no time; but did as her stepsister advised and stepped into the little hut.

When she entered, she saw an old woman sitting there on a bench, so enfeebled by age that her head shook.

The princess spoke to her in her usual friendly way: 'Good evening, mother. May I ask you for a drink of water?'

'You are heartily welcome to it,' said the old woman. 'Who may you be, that step beneath my lowly roof and greet me in so winning a way?'

The king's daughter told her who she was, and that she had gone out to relieve her heart in order to forget her great grief.

'And what may your great grief be?' asked the old woman.

'No doubt it is my fate to grieve,' said the princess, 'and I can never be happy again. I have lost my only love, and God alone knows whether I shall ever see him again.'

And she also told her why it was, and the tears ran down her cheeks in streams, so that anyone would have felt sorry for her.

When she had ended the old woman said: 'You did well in confiding your sorrow to me. I have lived long and may be able to give you a bit of good advice. When you leave here, you will see a lily growing from the ground. This lily is not like other lilies, however, but has many strange virtues. Run quickly over to it and pick it. If you can do that then you need not worry, for then one will appear who will tell you what to do.'

Then they parted and the king's daughter thanked her and went her way; while the old woman sat on the bench and wagged her head. But the queen's daughter had been standing without the hut the entire time, vexing herself, and grumbling because the king's daughter had taken so long.

So, when the latter stepped out, she had to listen to all sorts of abuse from her stepsister, as was to be expected. Yet she paid no attention to her and thought only of how she might find the flower of which the old woman had spoken. They went through the forest, and suddenly she saw a beautiful white lily growing in their very path. She was much pleased and ran up at once to pick it; but that very moment it disappeared and reappeared somewhat further away.

The king's daughter was now filled with eagerness, no longer listened to her stepsister's calls, and kept right on running; yet each time when she stooped to pick the lily, it suddenly disappeared and reappeared somewhat further away. Thus, it went for some time, and the princess was drawn further and further into the deep forest. But the lily continued to stand, and disappear and move further away, and each time the flower seemed larger and more beautiful than before.

At length, the princess came to a high hill, and as she looked toward its summit, there stood the lily high on the naked rock, glittering as white and radiant as the brightest star. The king's daughter now began to climb the hill, and in her eagerness, she paid no attention to stones nor steepness.

And when at last she reached the summit of the hill, lo and behold! The lily no longer evaded her grasp; but remained where it was, and the princess stooped and picked it and hid it in her bosom, and so heartfelt was her happiness that she forgot her stepsisters and everything else in the world.

For a long time, she did not tire of looking at the beautiful flower. Then she suddenly began to wonder what her stepmother would say when she came home after having remained out so long. And she looked around, in order to find the way back to the castle. But as she looked around, behold, the sun had set, and no more than a little strip of daylight rested on the summit of the hill. Below her lay the forest, so dark and shadowed that she had no faith in her ability to find the homeward path.

And now she grew very sad, for she could think of nothing better to do than to spend the night on the hilltop. She seated herself on the rock, put her hand to her cheek, cried, and thought of her unkind stepmother and stepsisters, and of all the harsh words she would have to endure when she returned. And she thought of her father, the king, who was away at war, and of the love of her heart, whom she would never see again; and she grieved so bitterly that she did not even know she wept.

Night came, and darkness, and the stars rose, and still the princess sat in the same spot and wept. And while she sat there, lost in her thoughts, she heard a voice say: 'Good evening, lovely maiden! Why do you sit here so sad and lonely?'

She stood up hastily, and felt much embarrassed, which was not surprising.

When she looked around, there was nothing to be seen but a tiny old man, who nodded to her and seemed to be very humble.

She answered: 'Yes, it is no doubt my fate to grieve, and never be happy again. I have lost my dearest love, and now I have lost my way in the forest and am afraid of being devoured by wild beasts.'

'As to that,' said the old man, 'you need have no fear. If you will do exactly as I say, I will help you.'

This made the princess happy; for she felt that all the rest of the world had abandoned her.

Then the old man drew out flint and steel and said: 'Lovely maiden, you must first build a fire.'

She did as he told her, gathered moss, brush and dry sticks, struck sparks and lit such a fire on the hill-top that the flame blazed up to the skies.

That done the old man said: 'Go on a bit and you will find a kettle of tar and bring the kettle to me.'

This the king's daughter did.

The old man continued: 'Now put the kettle on the fire.'

And the princess did that as well.

When the tar began to boil, the old man said: 'Now throw your white lily into the kettle.'

The princess thought this a harsh command, and earnestly begged to be allowed to keep the lily.

But the old man said: 'Did you not promise to obey my every command? Do as I tell you or you will regret it.'

The king's daughter turned away her eyes and threw the lily into the boiling tar; but it was altogether against her will, so fond had she grown of the beautiful flower.

The moment she did so, a hollow roar, like that of some wild beast, sounded from the forest. It came nearer, and turned into such a terrible howling that all the surrounding hills echoed it.

Finally, there was a cracking and breaking among the trees, the bushes were thrust aside, and the princess saw a great grey wolf come running out of the forest and straight up the hill. She was much frightened and would gladly have run away, had she been able.

But the old man said: 'Make haste, run to the edge of the hill and the moment the wolf comes along, upset the kettle on him!'

The princess was terrified, and hardly knew what she was about; yet she did as the old man said, took the kettle, ran to the edge of the hill, and poured its contents over the wolf just as he was about to run up.

And then a strange thing happened: no sooner had she done so than the wolf was transformed, cast off his thick grey pelt, and in place of the horrible wild beast, there stood a handsome young man, looking up to the hill. And when the king's daughter collected herself and looked at him, she saw that it was really and truly her lover, who had been turned into a werewolf.

It is easy to imagine how the princess felt. She opened her arms, and could neither ask questions nor reply to them, so moved and delighted was she. But the prince ran hastily up the hill, embraced her tenderly, and thanked her for delivering him.

Nor did he forget the little old man, but thanked him with many civil expressions for his powerful aid. Then they sat down together on the hilltop and had a pleasant talk. The prince told how he had been turned into a wolf, and of all he had suffered while running about in the forest; and the princess told of her grief, and the many tears she had shed while he had been gone. So, they sat the whole night through, and never noticed it until the stars grew pale and it was light enough to see.

When the sun rose, they saw that a broad path led from the hill-top straight to the royal castle; for they had a view of the whole surrounding country from the hilltop.

Then the old man said: 'Lovely maiden, turn around! Do you see anything out yonder?'

'Yes,' said the princess, 'I see a horseman on a foaming horse, riding as fast as he can.'

Then the old man said: 'He is a messenger sent on ahead by the king your father. And your father with all his army is following him.'

That pleased the princess above all things, and she wanted to descend the hill at once to meet her father.

But the old man detained her and said: 'Wait a while, it is too early yet. Let us wait and see how everything turns out.'

Time passed and the sun was shining brightly, and its rays fell straight on the royal castle down below.

Then the old man said: 'Lovely maiden, turn around! Do you see anything down below?'

'Yes,' replied the princess, 'I see a number of people coming out of my father's castle, and some are going along the road, and others into the forest.'

The old man said: 'Those are your stepmother's servants. She has sent some to meet the king and welcome him; but she has sent others to the forest to look for you.'

At these words, the princess grew uneasy and wished to go down to the queen's servants.

But the old man withheld her and said: 'Wait a while and let us first see how everything turns out.'

More time passed, and the king's daughter was still looking down the road from which the king would appear, when the old man said: 'Lovely maiden, turn around! Do you see anything down below?'

'Yes,' answered the princess, 'there is a great commotion in my father's castle, and they are hanging it with black.'

The old man said: 'That is your stepmother and her people. They will assure your father that you are dead.'

Then the king's daughter felt bitter anguish, and she implored from the depths of her heart: 'Let me go, let me go, so that I may spare my father this anguish!'

But the old man detained her and said: 'No, wait, it is still too early. Let us first see how everything turns out.'

Again, time passed, the sun lay high above the fields, and the warm air blew over meadow and forest. The royal maid and youth still sat on the hilltop with the old man, where we had left them.

Then, they saw a little cloud rise against the horizon, far away in the distance, and the little cloud grew larger and larger, and came nearer and nearer along the road, and as it moved one could see it was agleam with weapons, and nodding helmets, and waving flags, one could hear the rattle of swords, and the neighing of horses, and finally recognize the banner of the king.

It is not hard to imagine how pleased the king's daughter was, and how she insisted on going down and greeting her father.

But the old man held her back and said: 'Lovely maiden, turn around! Do you see anything happening at the castle?'

'Yes,' answered the princess, 'I can see my stepmother and stepsisters coming out, dressed in mourning, holding white kerchiefs to their faces, and weeping bitterly.'

The old man answered: 'Now they are pretending to weep because of your death. Wait just a little while longer. We have not yet seen how everything will turn out.'

After a time, the old man said again: 'Lovely maiden, turn around! Do you see anything down below?'

'Yes,' said the princess, 'I see people bringing a black coffin – now my father is having it opened. Look, the queen and her daughters are down on their knees, and my father is threatening them with his sword!'

Then the old man said: 'Your father wished to see your body, and so your evil stepmother had to confess the truth.'

When the princess heard that, she said earnestly: 'Let me go, let me go, so that I may comfort my father in his great sorrow!'

But the old man held her back and said: 'Take my advice and stay here a little while longer. We have not yet seen how everything will turn out.'

Again, time went by, and the king's daughter and the prince and the old man were still sitting on the hilltop.

Then the old man said: 'Lovely maiden, turn around! Do you see anything down below?'

'Yes,' answered the princess, 'I see my father and my stepsisters and my stepmother with all their following moving this way.'

The old man said: 'Now they have started out to look for you. Go down and bring up the wolf's pelt in the gorge.'

The king's daughter did as he told her.

The old man continued: 'Now stand at the edge of the hill.' And the princess did that, too. Now, one could see the queen and her daughters coming along the way and stopping just below the hill.

Then the old man said: 'Now throw down the wolf's pelt!' The princess obeyed him and threw down the wolf's pelt according to his command. It fell directly on the evil queen and her daughters. And then a most wonderful thing happened: no sooner had the pelt touched the three evil women than they immediately changed shape, and turning into three horrible werewolves, they ran away as fast as they could into the forest, howling dreadfully.

No more had this happened, than the king himself arrived at the foot of the hill with his whole retinue. When he looked up and recognized the princess, he could not at first believe his eyes; but stood motionless, thinking her a vision.

Then the old man cried: 'Lovely maiden, now hasten, run down and make your father happy!'

There was no need to tell the princess twice. She took her lover by the hand, and they ran down the hill.

When they came to the king, the princess ran on ahead, fell on her father's neck, and wept with joy. And the young prince wept as well, and the king himself wept; and their meeting was a pleasant sight for everyone.

There was great joy and many embraces, and the princess told of her evil stepmother and stepsisters and of her lover, and all that she had suffered, and of the old man who had helped them in such a wonderful way. But when the king turned around to thank the old man, he had completely vanished, and from that day on no one could say who he had been or what had become of him.

The king and his whole retinue now returned to the castle, where the king had a splendid banquet prepared, to which he invited all the able and distinguished people throughout the kingdom and bestowed his daughter on the young prince. And the wedding was celebrated with gladness and music and amusements of every kind for many days. I was there, too, and when I rode through the forest I met a wolf with two young wolves, and they showed me their teeth and seemed very angry.

And I was told they were none other than the evil stepmother and her two daughters.

From: The Swedish Fairy Book

Finis

Workbooks From The Scheherazade Foundation

We hope that you have enjoyed this collection of stories, gleaned from varying cultural corners of the world, and that you have been entertained by them.

But, have you considered the deeper meanings and interwoven layers that lie hidden beneath the surface?

At The Scheherazade Foundation, we believe that Teaching-Stories contain wisdom, information, and marvels that have the power to transform the way we think, and thereby change our lives.

Employed as a bedrock of culture throughout the centuries – challenging established patterns of thinking, while passing on knowledge and values – tales such as the ones contained in this volume are a rich resource ready and waiting to be mined.

As an aid to help in the perception of less-obvious facets and layers, we have created a series of original Workbooks. Aimed at stimulating thought-provoking discussions and igniting deep reflection, these tools will assist in unlocking the power of Teaching-Stories.

www.ingramcontent.com/pod-product-compliance
Lightning Source LLC
Chambersburg PA
CBHW030611310726
48979CB00003B/661

* 9 7 8 1 9 1 5 3 1 1 4 3 6 *